GLASS GRAPES
AND OTHER STORIES

Other books by Martha Ronk

Poetry

Chapbooks

Memoir

Glass Grapes
and Other Stories

✺

Martha Ronk

" Ronk

AMERICAN READER SERIES, NO. 10

BOA EDITIONS, LTD. ✺ ROCHESTER, NY ✺ 2008

First Edition
08 09 10 11   7 6 5 4 3 2 1

For information about permission to reuse any material from this book
please contact The Permissions Company at www.permissionscompany.
com or e-mail permdude@eclipse.net.

Publications by BOA Editions, Ltd.—a not-for-profit corporation under
section 501 (c) (3) of the United States Internal Revenue Code—are made
possible with funds from a variety of sources, including public funds from
the New York State Council for the Arts, a state agency; the Literature Program of the National Endowment for the Arts; the County of Monroe, NY;
the Lannan Foundation for support of the Lannan Translations Selection
Series; the Sonia Raiziss Giop Charitable Foundation; the Mary S. Mulligan
Charitable Trust; the Rochester Area Community Foundation; the Arts &
Cultural Council for Greater Rochester; the Steeple-Jack Fund; the Ames-
Amzalak Memorial Trust in memory of Henry Ames, Semon Amzalak
and Dan Amzalak; the TCA Foundation; and contributions from many
individuals nationwide. See Colophon on page 216 for special individual
acknowledgments.

Cover Design: Steve Smock
Interior Design and Composition: Richard Foerster
Manufacturing: Thomson-Shore
BOA Logo: Mirko

Library of Congress Cataloging-in-Publication Data

Ronk, Martha Clare.
  Glass grapes : stories / by Martha Ronk. — 1st ed.
    p. cm. — (American reader series ; no. 10)
  ISBN 978–1–934414–13–2 (pbk.)
  I. Title.

PS3568.O574G57 2008
813'.54–dc22

2008019126

BOA Editions, Ltd.
Nora A. Jones, Executive Director/Publisher
Thom Ward, Editor/Production
Peter Conners, Editor/Marketing
Glenn William, BOA Board Chair
A. Poulin, Jr., Founder (1938–1996)
250 North Goodman Street, Suite 306
Rochester, NY 14607
www.boaeditions.org

NATIONAL
ENDOWMENT
FOR THE ARTS

State of the Arts

NYSCA

Contents

—∞— *Part 3* —∞—

—∞—

Something obsessive about "l'objet" (the object) much too deep for anything rational quite possible.

—Joseph Cornell

Part 1

The Watch

I fainted trying to explain to his mother he really believed in revolution and God, that he really did think what he thought. I see myself lying on the linoleum floor in her kitchen, my knees splayed out. *God*, I said, looking up, *he's acting for God*. I knew it was wrong to lock him up and give him shock treatments, see his ideals as mere mania. Besides I believed that he was a sort of holy man or not exactly that and not that I really believed it, but sort of.

And the times were right, revolutionary and fervent, and he was ill, far beyond my ability to know it. There were the voices he heard, voices he talked to without sleeping for days on end and without anyone's being there, so he was ill they said and so I would say now, but for me then the voices were not something that had to be feared or cured or locked up. His hands are what I remember, how he picked them raw as if his eyes hurt so badly he had to distract himself, but then all I could see were his eyes. Paintings I'd not yet seen now get

11

in the way, but then I just looked back, indulgent and culpable. He was, as first loves are, what was. I couldn't stand back at a distance; I didn't know how, even as now I don't know how to get hold of a time when I was someone else.

Was I ill as well? All I remember is the smell of paint and the sort of dizzy nausea I felt painting the white fence around my parents' house, a task arranged to keep me busy, to keep my mind occupied, and it takes forever, each picket needing to be sanded and primed and painted with oily white paint, the smell of the paint and the heat of the August days making me dazed and off-balance. All the while I knew that the shape of the universe as I knew it was up to me and simultaneously that I was too weak and amorphous to shape anything. The smell of the fumes was overwhelming. I loved this man, spoke in echoes with him, followed him about without knowing it. They said he was mad. If he was mad I needed to do something, yet could do nothing. Instead, I did what I was told to do and I painted the inside of the pickets with a tiny brush, perfectly, stroke by stroke and prayed for the best.

If mechanical effort, limited and compulsive, could have made a difference, it would have. If unspoken and fervent thoughts could have helped, mine would have. I painted and held my breath against the paint fumes, held myself into a tight fist. I thought I was something filmy, caught and held. When September came, I kept studying, moving from classroom to classroom, in

The Watch

mechanized movements I thought would help, if not now, then later.

Later he was released from the hospital and moved to a small industrial town on the east coast not far from the sea. Some years passed. My life went elsewhere, no more certain, but ticking along as lives do in other cities, other streets. It was, I imagine, near sunset. He stood on the rocks by the sea for a long time, teetering and unsure. He asked about the injustice of it all. He used to dance, I could see him, like a puppet unstrung; he used to make noises from his throat as if he could find a sound to call forth an echoed response. The sun was setting behind his figure and he cast long shadows over the rocks. The rocks were wet and covered in moss. I don't know if this is what really happened, but I always see this scene as if it were true.

It was this particular event in my life—the image of him on the rocks and I elsewhere in the car—that seems to have determined all else. At this very moment in time I lost the watch he had given me, and so, once I had lost the watch in the gutter, I knew not only what had happened on the rocks by the sea and that I was to blame, but also that my fate was sealed. The watch slithered off my arm as I was closing the car door. I can't now remember where we were, but the person driving was just shifting gears, the stench of garbage was in the air, and I was pulling on the door handle. I am pulling on the handle in that vivid lost-time manner in which one tries to go back to recover what actually happened in the seconds during which something was said, something was lost, the universe tilted and the watch was off my wrist and into the gutter.

We never found it. We looked right at the spot where it should have fallen and couldn't see a thing. It wasn't something we went back to look for and couldn't find because someone else had. We looked right then, right away, the car at a forty-five degree angle to the curb as we were just pulling away slowly into the alley, and I said, *Stop! I've lost my watch*, but it had disappeared into that very second during which the car began to move. As the car moved forward at that slight angle, the watch broke, although neither of us heard anything, and slid into the overlap of the planes that define time, barely squeezing through just as I looked over at the driver who had a three-day growth of beard. This is very clear to me and fixed, his face and the three-day growth of beard. And in that frozen moment I saw that he, the man in the hospital who had given it to me, had completely lost himself to madness, stumbling off the rocks and drowning in the sea. I saw this scene as a freeze-frame, given to me again and again, unchanged and certain.

On the back of the watch was an inscription in Chinese ideograms: clarity. It stood for my middle name in some transliterated way I couldn't understand. But it wasn't true. I wasn't clear. I was muddled and confused, as if standing by the jeweled staircase with dew on my stockings and the moon just sliding beneath the clouds, immoral and lost. *The jeweled steps are already*

The Watch

quite white with dew, / It is so late that the dew soaks my
gauze stockings, / And I let down the crystal curtain / And
watch the moon through the clear autumn.

Even the man with the three-day growth realized
that something had occurred, not to him and not to me,
but to some more far reaching state of things. I married the man with the beard who had been witness to
the event as if I could by such an act hang onto the one
who had died as well as to the man in the car and could
collapse two into one, past into present. I went along
blindly, living a kind of palimpsest until the man I had
married realized I wasn't married to him at all but was
reaching through him to the past, not so much living a
life as living an image of a life. Once he realized this,
he took up with another woman and then another and
another as if it would undo the awful lock the situation
had on us, but it only made things worse.

After he left, I took a job as a house painter in the
seaside city where the man had died. Although I hadn't
actually been there, I thought I could imagine what it
must have been like for him to walk these streets, stop
in these corner stores, talk to these people. I dreamed
endless dreams of tracking him down, following his foot-
steps, talking to friends and lovers, reading his diaries,
writing my words on top of his. I wrote letters to those
who had known him and read letters he had written to
me, airmail letters on blue foldout paper, and practiced
speaking in his voice, saying his phrases, using his
flashcards for learning Chinese. I took up memorizing

ideograms by carrying the small cards about with me and flipping through them while I waited in line or waited to fall asleep. Moving my fingers on the squares of cardboard, the edges and grainy surfaces, was like eating. I took small jobs repainting single rooms, a bedroom here, a living room there. In between I'd sit by the ladder, pull up my knees, and read the cards, holding them in my hands and turning them over and over tracing the black lines, resting my painted thumb on the bottom edge of the card, staring.

Eventually he appeared to me, at first in dreams in which I followed his heavy woolen coat around New Haven, in and out of cobbled streets, up and down steps, in and out of apartment buildings, around and around like a man lost in the crowd. Just as I'd catch a glimpse, he'd disappear, and I'd wake in a sweat, smelling of rancid butter, the smell I always associated with him, and I'd know I'd gotten close. Once I got to lean into him in the dream, to feel his body against mine and I knew it was what I had been waiting for and would keep on waiting for.

About a year later when I was walking home for lunch, he appeared in person in the shadow of a rock near the New Haven library. He was faded and damp but I knew him. I always knew he'd come back to the city where he'd lost touch with himself. People told me I'd had a hallucination, that I was overworked and ill from paint fumes, quite ill in fact and should do something about it, but it wasn't like that. He asked me what time it was as if he were late. Since I didn't have a watch, I couldn't tell him. We spoke as ordinary people would passing on the street. During the years in which he appeared, always hurrying and always a bit faded, I was content. I knew that although I couldn't force it, he would eventually show up, we'd talk in the frank manner we had always talked, and I'd go on. There was nothing particularly exalted about it. Rather it felt reassuring in some way I can't explain. I asked him if he would come again and he promised he would and he did many times and then he didn't.

Sometimes I began to imagine myself as the person who found the watch in the gutter, someone who was, perhaps, decisive; she picked it up, knew her luck, changed her name and now runs a public radio station in Santa Barbara. She believes in herself, her work, the impeccable clarity of her vision. I have seen her walking to work; her step, decisive and quick, her heels clicking on the cement sidewalks that run along the sea.

The Tea Bowl

He: The mind is utterly unlike the body.
She: My eyes itch. I can't think.
He: Don't touch them, I keep telling you, don't touch them,
and don't think about it.

Sometimes my skin just gives way. It started when I was a child—rashes, bumps, patches of eczema and itches—violent as internal storms which accompanied them. I was miserable or it was Christmas. A bottle of perfumed cream appeared in my stocking. It meant, my mother said, the promise one day of perfect beauty and love and I spread it over my entire body, head to toe.

In the morning I couldn't open my eyes. My face was a moon and I couldn't stop scratching. I think that year I got a pogo stick but I was ill or worse. The outside moved inside and then appeared again on the outside, my skin aflame. My mother lit up a Lucky Strike and went out.

When I was sent away to boarding school I swelled up again. I was terrified and ugly. At home I kept myself tethered by memorizing the exact placement of each item in the room, the fifteen steps measured off from doorway to wall, the number of irregular roses in the wallpaper I counted again and again to make sure. Here nothing was certain. The unfamiliar pulsed around me. I wanted to get out of there, get away.

In those days the kind nurses in the infirmary shrugged vacantly and applied witch hazel compresses to everything: pregnancy, the desire of girls for girls, bulimia. They lay damp compresses across my face, wound them around and around my itchy neck. I was the Magritte painting, a head wrapped in swaddling clothes.

My husband says the mind and body aren't connected. At night I rubbed his back as he lay on his side and breathed and breathed, in and out, in and out. I anchored myself by this vast expanse of back and skin. *Don't touch me*, he said.

I've never told anyone about how when I was seven I concentrated and slowly slid my foot through the wall. Such events are different from visions because the dead, I think, decide of their own accord whether to appear or not. I miss the vision of my mother's ghost hanging barefoot over the backyard, her silk dress blowing in the breeze, her hair recently permed, the brave insouciance of it, but I know also that this wafting was her choosing, not mine.

It was always in the downstairs lavatory that I tried it. I tapped with my tennis shoe, sometimes hard, sometimes soft, and sometimes I scuffed up the wall and had to sneak back later with Ajax so no one would suspect. But one time when I was concentrating but pretending not to, the toe of my foot just blurred into the realm on the other side of the wall, no falling or tumbling, just the slightest of movements into something not the room I was in.

It was Christmas and I could hear my mother crying in the kitchen, the mashed potatoes soggy with her tears, salty and wetter and miserable for us all who had to eat them. We sat feeling lumpy and dismissed. She lit up a Lucky and went out, slamming the door.

He said, *Don't touch me. Leave me alone. Just keep your hands to yourself,* he said. I tucked my hands up under my own knees, curled up around my own body at the edge of the bed. I began having those small itches that are the signs of something. At first you think they are simply mosquito bites, but there are too many, they are too small, it is the wrong season and the ponds have dried up.

It's two thousand and four, he yelled. The coffee came up in the espresso pot. I scratched my arms. He scalded the milk. *It's two thousand and four and what have we come to.* His voice grew louder. I burned my tongue. I couldn't get what was being said. I couldn't come awake and took in only occasional words. I popped antihistamines and drank coffee. The rash crept down my arms and legs and between my fingers and toes. I tried to stop up my ears, not to listen to my skin, not to hear I was floating out in the pond like the fake island of algae and moss and looking deceptively like a real island, growing grasses and trees and moving peculiarly hither and thither across Whitingham Pond. I wanted what had been promised me at Christmas. He went out and slammed the door.

Last summer at the train station in Brattleboro I met a boy who was beautiful and aged in some unfathomable way the very young take on, like his grandfather, who, although in his seventies continued to be virile and vain, combing his fingers through his thick hair. But he was in the wrong body for his shyness, and, although he looked much older, was only fourteen, mis-sized like shoes one can't help buying because they are beautiful and one will never get to New York with the same amount of money again or will never be again in the mood for yellow shoes, but they are too small or too big, but you can't help buying them, and then, of course, they hurt and won't stay put and slide up and down on the back of the heel until one has to give them up, although one can't give them up because they are brand new, and so puts them in a drawer for another time when conditions will be different.

Perhaps, one thinks afterwards, if only the landscape had been rearranged, phone lines multiplied, different people invited to dinner, other careers taken on, and not that one evening, whatever one evening it happens to be. Things have gotten out of hand and you try to head them off at the pass, to turn them round, but it's useless.

There's no turning back, none at all, no way to get up and take up the game of cowboys and Indians where you left off years ago before lunch. The wooden slip bead on the cowboy hat I used to slide up and down with distracted pleasure when I ran about the backyard of my childhood is cracked in two. It has vanished into the thin air of the past. It ought to be sitting on my dresser in the morning. I ought to be eight. I can hear her crying in the kitchen. I can hear the door slam.

He moved out after I finished the essay on Japanese noodle cups for a new design magazine. Perhaps it was the wrong decision. Perhaps we had delayed the decision too long. What, one wonders, is "too long." There's the decision itself, and there is all that surrounds it like the space inside and outside the bowl, the air around which the clay clings, the space of the white porcelain against which the brush strokes sketch in pagodas, persimmons, dragonflies, drifting clouds. The noodle cup sits perfectly in the palm of a hand.

I couldn't open my eyes. I put ice over my crusted lids. I did every incantation I could think of, swallowed so many antihistamines I walked about in a daze, bumped into door frames, fell asleep in the afternoon, couldn't wake up in the morning. I sprayed my nose and lay compresses across my forehead. *Were you hyperactive as a child*, the shrink asks. *Were you given medication to*

*slow you down, keep you from throwing yourself against
the wall?*

I rode the bike with wooden blocks on the pedals
for five hours every day or I rocked madly in the corner
of the room. *Just get out of here, go out, go run around the
block five times*, my mother said. I broke things. Even
today when I walk into a room I look first of all for the
breakables and try to move as slowly as possible. Walk
on the bottom of the sea, I tell myself, go more slowly,
you will break it, it will fall to the ground in pieces. If
you turn a somersault into the French doors, the windows will cut your knees and you'll have scars for the
rest of your life, you will, I promise you, you will. If we
had collected teacups, if we had walked through the
antique mart and picked up suitcases covered in stick-
ers from foreign lands. If we'd moved somewhere; if the
bodies had behaved; if I hadn't been allergic; if it were
possible to hold air in one's hands. If only one could be
other than oneself, come in a body other than the one
one comes in. On some tea bowls the blue ink is deep
and almost black, on others so pale as to disappear into
the clay itself, pale as a line of inquiry, the to and fro
of a jagged line, broken as the bamboo broom I brought
home from Little Tokyo thinking to sweep with it and
leaving it abandoned in a shed.

Someone is hopping up and down on one foot. The
moon rises on the tea bowl. One man watches. One hides
his hands in the large folds of a gown. He is bald, he is
always bald. The noodle cup has been broken twice and

mended twice, once in the distant past with gold. *I want my life*, I said, *please*, I said. I threw out feather pillows, scoured for mold, wore only synthetic fibers, bought products whose labels I read and reread. I stopped using soap and splashed bottled water over my swollen face. I couldn't breathe. He moved out.

I wrote a long article on Memphis ware, clear bright glaze. It's one of my best pieces, often reprinted. I have a house filled with precious pottery. On every surface there is a bowl filled with air. In the background my mother stands at the counter and watches silently while we eat her mashed potatoes. The monk hops up and down, up and down. I move slowly as if I were underwater. I have perfect skin; everyone says so.

—◦◦◦—

Old Nylon Bathrobes

But she's so wonderful, he insisted, the man who was
my husband, and she was. When I am scrubbing things,
cleaning and tidying, sentences like this come back to
me as childish phrases stick in my mind and repeat
and repeat as if they would solve something or change
the course of events, *Doctor Foster went to Gloucester, in
a shower of rain; he stepped in a puddle up to his middle
and never went there again.* Sometimes the sentences
are incantatory to prevent what I hoped wouldn't happen, but that sometimes did. She was wonderful in that
offhand way that looks as giddy as a too-short summer
dress. But on her it looked as right as the bright day
lilies right there at the end of a corner lot dotted with
blowing scraps of newsprint and tires.

When I first met her, she was a teenager and hung
out in Porter Square kicking tires and smoking cigarettes and dope with a bunch of kids and Rog. He was
the only one whose name I remember because she took

up with him later, before or after my husband I can't recall, or won't, the memory stuck in the off position, I guess. Her father worked at the See's Candy factory, you could smell burning sugar from blocks away, although I never saw him there, only imagined the chocolate dollops on a conveyer belt, and saw him in fact only once before he died. He was on Disability and at home, thin and looking even thinner in a worn nylon bathrobe with amoeba squiggles all over it like the ones that ran all over the Formica in my childhood bathroom which I attempted to count more times than I can remember so I wouldn't have to worry about growing hair or breasts or unmanageable desires which kept sneaking up in cars late at night. If I could only count them all, put them in some sort of scheme or pattern, although of course the whole was designed to resist pattern and not to show the dirt.

He was very ill by then and too frail to rein her in or even see her clearly. Her blond hair stood out like light streaks in that battered room with its battered stuffed furniture here and there and even on the porch. It has always seemed to me the saddest state of all, the smell of outdoor stuffed chairs, never drying out from the damp winter through the whole of the hot summer. When you sit in them you feel old yourself, as if they would pull you into the undertow, envelope and surround in a way that in normal circumstances might be comforting, but in this particular case is not.

Old Nylon Bathrobes

I stared at his bathrobe so I didn't have to think about fate, his or mine or hers, and I thought about the one I wore in a house that smelled the same, moldy and mildewed in the days when all of us thought it was cool to wear secondhand clothes, when we were young enough to toss on thrift-store shirts and look just fine, when I thought there was plenty of time and that everything would, if I waited long enough, shape up. My bathrobe was black with faded roses, my husband's was light blue and he wore it even in the darkroom so that it smelled of fixer, a smell I hadn't thought of for years until I walked into a store in Riverside to pick up recent prints and there he was, my husband, in his blue nylon bathrobe smelling of fixer and invading my mind.

The bathrobes painted by Jim Dine suggest inchoate gender, although why I'm not sure, except as they are like the bathrobes themselves, covering, uncovering, *Frosted Night Robe III* glistening with white chalk, the body beneath it white and overripe.

The Woodcut Bathrobe was begun as a single color lithograph; from this print he traced the outline of the robe. He then cut his tracing into sections and had pieces of plywood cut to match these patterns. After each wooden section was inked a different color, the plywood robe was reassembled. A Sheet of Natsume paper was relief-printed by hand by rubbing with a spoon from the back.

They hang in the pictures like sad flags, although someone who knows me well says that I say that because my childhood was sad and therefore I am sad and project it onto everything. If this sort of causality is true we might as well give up, don't you think, not that I would argue for much human agency, but a modicum, at least, even once in a while would be fine. My husband's sexuality wasn't inchoate, I don't think, a bit promiscuous perhaps, but not inchoate, indeed his gender a sort of gift he might have said, even to me. And we all are given or not given gifts, of course, her blond hair, for example, glowing there in the dim room while her father was thinning and dying.

Her mother had disappeared years ago. Married right after the war, she then freaked out and left, back to Europe somewhere or wherever she went in a babushka, folded into a neat triangle and tied under her chin, her resolve to get away, out of their poverty and sagging chairs, not what she had imagined America would be, leaving two children behind with a man who tried to give them to relatives who wouldn't taken them. They found the girl already so truant that after he died, they took her in for only a short while and then gave up, sending her back to be truant in her own neighborhood which is how my husband taking photographs in the parking lot came across her.

There they were, those kids, leaning into cars, not their own, but leaning into them nonetheless in the way of adolescents as if cars provided the ancestral

Old Nylon Bathrobes

hearth missing everywhere else. And my husband, the photographer, saw all this and found her wonderful, vivid and blond and wising off, which he loved more than anything in those days. In those days he too was on the edge and liked his own explosive and dramatic hyperstates, hugged them to him like silk wrapped around and tied about the waist. He liked complete irreverence and what he disliked about me was that I was tidy, scrubbing and cleaning and making doctor's appointments and scheduling things and formulating plans in my Week-At-A-Glance, despite how young I was, buying practical shoes and marching off to work.

Some people hate going to work, but I'm not one of them. I'm grateful to have someplace to go where I can tick off items accomplished, but these things make some people crazy and so his finding at random a girl with vast enthusiasm for sex and drugs and rock-and-roll was everything he hoped for and everything he wanted on the other side of his camera. She took so many drugs so often she had to crash at our apartment, arriving at two A.M. in a state that demanded immediate attention, most of it from me, he taking photographs from various angles and with various flash attachments there in the hallway as I recall, although I can't seem to locate any of the pictures, certain as I am that I put them carefully in orange boxes on the top shelf of the closet.

Like any good mother, I made her warm milk and bananas, wrapped her in bathrobes and blankets, while she told stories in rapid fire, hiccoughing and laughing until the room filled up with it and crying like a child and then almost ready to sleep, but he wanted the gory details so she'd comply, not, to her credit, particularly interested in reliving the night, but she knew she had a safe place to crash, and she was willing to pay. I actually think people should be allowed some privacy, but of course he was a photographer, a voyeur already in place and wanted to know how many tabs or snorts, how many boys, how many cups of coffee even though you'd think this bit wouldn't be of interest but for him everything was of interest, the all-night cafés and the girl with the multiple earrings and the tiny turquoise bra and the endless cups of coffee. It was his love of Bartók got me, the aching and percussive harshness. The attraction is that men are so dependent and assertive at the same time, so full of rights and vulnerabilities, of enthusiasm and collapse. They sweep one along like leaves, thinking is out of the question.

When I returned from work one day the apartment was transformed by shopping carts. They had pushed ten or so over from the Star Market and decorated them all with crepe paper and hung balloons and put Christmas wrapping paper over all the white walls and Bartók's *Music for Strings, Percussion and Celesta* was blaring and it was my birthday they said, although it wasn't, she of the bright hair, my husband, the car kids and clearly it had been going on all day and how could I refuse. One tried saying no, I can't go along, really I can't, I'm sure it would be grand, I'm tired, been on my feet all day, but

Old Nylon Bathrobes

there was no way not to join in. It was, they said, my birthday. I sat in a chair like a convict waiting for the explosions to stop, for her blond hair to stop sprouting, for everyone to stop eating the blue icing on the cake, for the nausea to pass, the drugs to have had their day.

Later one walks from one room to the other, in the bathrobe designed for such walking from here to there or from sleep to waking or from waking to getting, as they used to do in black and white movies, to bed with the pulled-down sheets, tightly tucked hospital corners my mother used to make me do on all the beds. After they'd left, I found myself walking mechanically about, repeating phrases and snatches of song, moving farther and farther back into the dark house, shutting off lights and curling into corners until I found the right one, the best one always turning out to be the one in back of the clothes in the closet, up on a wide plank of a shelf where I had a collection of buttons and bits of cloth that had been torn up for rags kept in the back closet for waxing furniture and dusting moldings. I'd done it as a child, and I did it again. I sat for hours in the dark before I got under the clean sheets and waited for the sound of the front door.

I didn't leave him after his affair with her, although perhaps I should have. It didn't then seem part of a pattern, just a painful lapse, just a having-been-taken-up, drawn in, unable to help himself, and perhaps it didn't even happen that time, although the fine line between rhapsody and the sheets is often very fine. But whatever it was, it was brief and seemingly uncomplex and I didn't allow myself to think about it so I'm as much to blame as anyone. I just didn't want him to go away. It's more than love. It's the being taken with the reality of another person, you just can't stop believing in it, though all the evidence tells you to turn him into an object. *Get over there on the shelf,* you want to say. *You are a frayed robe, go hang yourself up in the closet, your arms droop, your hem is uneven, you have no chest hair.* I said, *Can't we talk about it or get a therapist or find out what's wrong or something,* but he said, *Talking fucks up everything* and I knew he was right. I just couldn't help thinking there must be something to do, some way to fix it.

Some years later she disappeared into Mexico—lost and druggy, more of that fate, I'm afraid, playing itself out, although it happened years after I feared something bad might happen. No one's been able to find her. It was random, a one night of raucousness she hadn't planned for or counted on, or at least her boyfriend told me that, it just happened, *random-like* he said, as if there were no way to make more sense of it than that. *She just disappeared,* he said. *Where were you,* I accused, but he returned with familiar lassitude, *It doesn't matter really does it, it just happened,* he said and I thought, *If only you had or if only I had,* and then I stopped myself because there is no way of making any sense of it or of that life that comes into one's life in the human form that takes the air out of us.

But as anyone knows, descriptions don't match facts, but rather are made in the space hanging between, in

Old Nylon Bathrobes

this case the girl and my husband, who described her with hands, gestures, face, smile, and the bland phrase *she's so wonderful* which could never convey his being taken by her grit and giddiness, the way she leaned against the hood of the car, hooking one toe under and putting a hand on a hip to sway and pull at the knotted sash. My own awe was, of course, tempered by jealousy, not at her youth, since I wasn't so much older and didn't have much sense of what that might mean until years later, but by her way of plunging into things.

I might wish it were otherwise, might wish I were different, might even wish things had arranged themselves differently, but they hadn't. The fate of all of us seems determined, looking back as I am now, by that moment with her and him and the bathrobes. When I met her father in that collapsing dim room with the open boxes of half-eaten chocolates, I saw her fate written on the bathrobe he was wearing, everything contained in paisley scrawl: her fate, his fate, my own perhaps. There's a pattern I've come to see behind everything that happens—nothing psychological or traumatic, but a pattern etched somehow in the objects one encounters so that everything has to turn out as it does. If it were only aesthetic, I suppose, we wouldn't mind the power of objects so much; if it were just the making of a pattern, concave, convex, light and shade, the positive and the negative space in a painting by Jim Dine, but, of course, it never is.

The Score

The man without memory remembered everything. He knew the dates especially for historical events that happened in The City, the name for the city of San Francisco. You don't understand, I said to my friend, it isn't that he doesn't remember, it is that he can will himself to forget. Now that's a gift most don't have, I mean not if you're not immoral or criminal. I mean, those guys might be different and I'm not talking different, just slightly. It's the kind of willpower you mostly get with ballplayers you know, I mean when you watch them you know that they can just will most anything.

My friend says yeah, run right up to the hoop fast as you can, and then just before you shoot, relax the hands. What I'm talking about, I said, except this guy's no ballplayer, way older and out of shape and it's like what you said, full speed ahead and then nothing, not a jot of a night that you had a conversation that changed your life and even his maybe and where does it all go, I asked, watching Kobe put it right through.

I ask the man without memory if he will talk to me about what he says he doesn't remember and he says it's no use, nothing's any use if you have to talk about it. The past is the past, he says. No use going over the past. I say, remember it was in the fifth year we were together and it was when we realized there'd be no time like the present and I'd get older, and then we'd just have the house and the dog even if we did get some other animals or something. I've seen other couples, I said, with more than one dog, three sometimes even in the small apartment, and walking them all in the park late on Sunday afternoons with the dying eucalyptus and the dust blowing up all around. Anyhow, even then we realized it would be later on soon enough, and then it'd all be carved out for us and we couldn't change it. You know those decisions that loom as substantial and are, even if you pretend they aren't and even if you pretend time will slow down because you want it to and you won't be left high and dry. You want everything in slow motion like walking to school on a snowy day when you lived where it snowed and time just seems to keep on being the same time for a long time.

Later he takes me to the oldest bar in North Beach and we sit there surrounded by wood and glass and Cinzano, gleaming red from the highest shelf, and he tells me about the baths near the pier and about the old guys in rubber caps who plunge in the icy cold in the winter, year after year. Now those are guys, he says. I say, could we go back over it please, and he says *of course* first, first he says *of course* before he talks about how he lost his wedding ring on the edge of a washstand in a gas station in North Dakota where he remembers the exact town and the exact date and wanted to fish it out of the drain but the attendant said no. And I say something about how he'd said *of course,* but then the moment has passed and after this we get to watching the game on the TV overhead and we just think then about the movement of the teams from one end to the other and neither of us says much or remembers anything but the score which changes from time to time in the small square at the bottom of the screen.

Glass Grapes

He knows I like things that break, and so the Indian pots and recently the thin glasses or vases hand-blown you can get from the antique store nearby or even, although this seems particularly useless and fragile, the glass fruits you find from time to time abandoned in the back in dusty bins: grapes, pears, apples. You hold their cool transparency in your hands. Yet for all their fragility they are there, straddling that imperceptible border between, well, being there and not. You can see them and in the case of tumblers, see through them. I especially like the pale green grapes, well almost anything that feels as if it could simply blow apart in your hands if you squeezed just a bit too hard, not on purpose, mind you, but just without thinking or without pretending to think. I have quite a collection now because he is good at finding whatever his object of affection seems to want. He has a gift of generosity, unable really not to think of what someone might like.

I've known people who can never think what to get for someone else or even those who can't think what to get for themselves and stand baffled at store counters, in malls, but he is, without really putting his mind to it, able to hit on just the right thing. He knew before I did that I liked things that were temporary and tangential, things that seemed about to evaporate and lift off, as if some particular view of life were being confirmed as I undid the paper wrappings. That's another of his gifts, really, his ability to size one up and know what one wants, to improve one's lot in life, to cook exactly the bit one would especially enjoy, to say exactly the right thing at a moment when things seem perfect already, to plan exactly the right outing for an occasion or to make an occasion when there isn't any. Most of my friends muddle along, forgetting sometimes or remembering to pick up a paperback for one's birthday, and I think of one of my favorite poems by Frank O'Hara where he tells which books he snatched for his hosts before getting on the 7:15 train, not the *New World Writing*, but Verlaine, all before Billie Holiday died and before he remembers leaning on the john at the 5 SPOT. He stopped breathing, listening to her sing.

I'm sitting on the stool in his kitchen, leaning on the marble counter with my drink, neat; I always take it neat. He's not home yet and he always makes dinner, so there's not much for me to do except balance on the stool, an uncomfortable if highly designed stool, and wait. I'm thinking and if it can be called thinking, thinking about this glass, glass grapes and other things. When I come home from work and classes, he's always made dinner and put flowers about and planned an extra something in the form of a caramelized pear for dessert and waiting for me to ask for something. Isn't there anything you want, he says, and he smiles the smile of the generous. He's younger than I am, but somehow despite that and my inability to reciprocate in kind, he's chosen me and all I have to do is figure out how to be grateful.

But I think, what is this generosity, you know how you wonder when you are drinking. What is it and what does it mean? Once I said I didn't need a camera but he said I would if I didn't at the moment, that I'd want to record a trip one day and then he arranged for the trip and indeed I was grateful as we traveled to Santa Fe to record the ruins and monuments and stones. I took pictures of pots, cracked, repaired, fissured. It was hard not to love him, so I did. No one had ever been so generous to me. In my own family the niggardly were viewed as the blessed and the meek were closer to God.

Mother hummed hymns while she did the dishes. So growing up I grew certain of the certitudes of giving up and cutting back. I have few clothes, but he, he has so many shirts you'd have to think of Gatsby and even on holiday he has suitcases full of shirts of so many colors and shades of the same color, so beautiful that like Daisy when I first saw them, I wanted to remember how to cry.

Why he is able to get it all right is beyond me and why he has chosen me as the recipient of all his efforts and special insights is also beyond me. I'm not any more attractive than the next person, certainly not in a category matching his own, and generally, except when the glow he projects is projected back at him, he must feel I'm a disappointment no matter how hard I try and, of course, I do try, anyone would, caught in the golden bubble of his generosity. And it's not as if he is simply extravagant as I've explained. No, he's deft and sensitive and gets me exactly what he is right to think I would want even, as I said before, before it is clear to me but then, of course, it is clear to me and he is absolutely right that I should have been wearing green, collecting glass grapes, going to school all along.

In psychological terms I'd have to say it is hard to figure him out, I mean why would anyone devote his life to it, and I hope simply to continue to be able to remain grateful. I wonder, though, in the back of my mind if I'll fail. I try, of course, to reciprocate in small ways with whatever means I can, a paperback here and a bottle of wine there. I replanted his indoor plants and saved up for a terra cotta pot for the ficus. And I'm happy to be grateful. But it can't be enough. Not that he would ever say so—he doesn't, I think, even notice the inequity—but that I am always behind. No matter what I contrive for him, I am always behind. He says he just likes to see me smile. Just likes to see me happy and I am happy, and smiling is the easiest thing in the world. He says life is just to be made a bit easier for those he loves and he does love me. He finds me charming and so long as I don't think about it, it's ok, but I worry, what if I forget to do it or can't be charming or try, one day, just a bit too hard so that it is altogether not charming but something else.

I couldn't ask for anything more or for more generosity or, and this is perhaps the most important, exquisite tact. He never overdoes it, really. He is careful to make sure that the gifts come when they should come or that they pick me up when I am blue, although I find lately that I rarely allow myself a mood for fear of eliciting a favor. He wants the world to be a good and beautiful place and he wants me to believe it. Some people want to construct faith in others. It is their purpose in life to get others to believe, in what I'm not exactly sure, but in something, not God perhaps but in the possibility of things, abundance and overflow. All this sounds, I'm sure you think, rather silly and superficial but I don't mean it that way. And it's not simply their good manners or lack of irony. It's more of a mission. The opposite of pulling the rug out from under you and we've all known those who do that.

He says I just haven't opened myself to the world. It's not that he imagines himself as virtuous; his efforts don't extend to institutions or even to theories about the distribution of wealth or to each according to his needs. He simply wants to straighten things up a bit in the corner he's been given. He's an optimist. He thinks things will work out for the best, even believes in progress, an idea I thought long ago relegated to the nineteenth century along with winged bronze statues. He takes pleasure in thinking up treats: raspberries and cream, apple tarts, glass grapes. He knows what each of us would like or would like to like if we thought about it.

I'm tired of thinking. The corners of my mouth are tired. I don't mind being grateful, certainly not. I *am* grateful. I try not to draw attention to myself or complain. If I should forget and ask for something, there it is, too large, too colorful, too exactly what I wanted sitting in front of me wrapped in tissue, spoken in soft tones, thrown about my shoulders. How can one possibly complain about getting what one wants. The small glass glints in the sun. So what if my position could be described by an outsider who can't possibly understand as compromised. Besides, whose isn't in some way or other? That's what I ask myself over and over again. I sit on the stool in the kitchen and review the possibilities. It's not as if I'm having to perform or even that he asks too often for me to be charming. I like to sit with a basket of glass in my lap. I do, I really do like it. I like to smile over at him while he's cutting things, apples and bananas for fruit salad, Cointreau and sugar over the top. I like to pick up the glass grapes and hold them to the light while I'm reading, a sort of dare really and in spite of my concentration on the book in front of me I haven't lost track yet, haven't broken any. Once one came loose and rolled to the floor, rolled into the corner and came to rest. I like to think sometimes of them breaking and then reforming as if the film were running backwards, as if they were dissolving into bits of light right in my hand and then molding ever so slowly into rounded shapes. The grapes are strung on a silver wire. There are eight of them.

Only once in a while and really never for very long do I feel as if I've been asked for more than is required, due him really. He is so much more generous than I, than I could ever be. And he understands the position I'm in, understood it really before I did. Yet, lately, sitting on this stool and drinking my drink, I've simply felt like being hateful. I have no cause. I wake in a bath of sunlight. Yet the idea of something petty and mean edges into view, you know, *just to do it*. Once I drove someone who loved me off by putting my hand through a window. There, I said, now you *have* to go away and I went by myself to the emergency room and had the glass picked out and the hand stitched up. It was a hateful thing to do. And the worst part was I was glad. That'll show him, I thought. That'll show them all. "I won't." But what I wouldn't is no longer clear to me, only the array of doctors and pills and endless, endless hours.

This time I'd rather not. It's such a price to pay for proving one's point. There are the sleepless nights and hallucinations and fear. I can't, I think, bear the little weasely shadows slithering the walls. Just to prove a point and what sort of point is it to prove really that one isn't charming, won't ever be charming, hates the idea of being charming. Or to prove that things are not rosy. What's the point of that, I ask myself when things

GLASS GRAPES

are rosy. He says that he's the best thing that's ever happened to me and I know he's right. I try to remember to smile as Patsy must have when Frank brought her the Verlaine. But I open my mouth and the corners crack. I wonder if I like green after all. I wonder if I like seeing through things so much. As a child, my mother says, I ate sand from the sandbox and refused lunch. I am sitting at the stool in the kitchen. On the radio for the anniversary of the moon landing the announcer plays an old tape of an astronaut from over thirty years ago reading from the Bible: "And God saw everything that he had made, and, behold, it was very good."

The Sofa

To choose to take someone into your life is an act of supreme willpower. It's a decision too large to contemplate, and I can't even get in the car without thinking about the moment between staying and leaving and dropping everything in a scatter on the garage floor and picking it up and wishing just to have to pick it up for some time so I don't have to decide anything else, but just concentrate on this one thing—keys and wallet and books, and the lipstick rolling under the wheels as it does.

On that very day of the lipstick my best friend decides to take a lover. She tells me about the joys of living with someone, the coziness of it all, and how he and she do this and that together, and shop and cook meals together, side by side, rhapsodic in the kitchen with the tile he bought from a wrecking company and put in himself. She's chosen him all right and says everything will be perfect, so she says. She says it is just as if it were all meant to be just as I am cramming everything back into my purse and getting in my car and closing the door.

I ask her via e-mail why she is so taken with this new arrangement and why, given her gifts at irony, she needs be so over-the-top. I mean she's not that young. She writes she is hurt by my questions and asks why I would do such a thing. But I ask, myself now, not her, what is this thing called love anyhow, what makes people choose each other in the first place, choose each other out of all the others they might choose and go about ordering dinners and designing kitchens with green concrete counters and picking out a car under fluorescent lights on a Friday night along the wide boulevard of cars and balloons and treat it as something fated. As if it were a given that you had to go hand in hand to an architecturally significant hotel and hole up for days poking around old neighborhoods looking for architecturally significant doorways or bridges or even the Toledo and Ohio Railroad station in Columbus as if you just had to.

Also I can't see eating with someone else on a regular basis, child or lover or whatever. It's so intrusive really I don't know why others choose to do it but they do. Kids throw food around and dinner is a disaster and lovers take note of your imperfections like closing your eyes when you're thinking hard about what to say until you can't eat then either. Perhaps, I think, people adopting other people is the definition of what it means to be

The Sofa

human or else I've lived too long by myself and although I realize this doesn't exactly follow I think it anyway. These people have taken on other people as if it were natural, or as if, despite its unnaturalness, they take it on and make it a fact, and then insist on it, either by full embrace or by elaborate questioning of what they have done, neither of which makes any difference since it is what they have done. She writes me a cryptic response and then signs off: *It was meant to be.*

What I think about these choices doesn't much matter since no one wants my opinion and since I have no lover or child of my own and wouldn't want to, really I wouldn't want to have anyone intruding in my daily life, I mean it's so hard to do the things one has to do without having to think about someone else. Yet I do think about them, because the choosing stands out, the arbitrary and insistent shape of it. Everything would have been so different if the choice hadn't been made. One might have written a book about brain surgery, arranged gazebos and Buddha heads in the back yard, made a documentary film about a mad gardener who wears bells on his shoes so as not to startle his neighbors at 4 A.M. when he comes to trim the bushes.

They've just come back from a trip, this couple, and have had good meals and a good time. The paintings in the museum interested one more than the other. One of them doesn't much care for architecture and I have to agree though no one asked me. Architecture is such an imposition on the world, too opinionated and abrupt, but again, if you've ever met an architect, you'll know what I mean. They take over corners like someone has moved in and camped out in your living room without thinking and pushed things around like the sofa so you can't recognize where you are anymore or even who you are, things are so rearranged and without even asking. Even your taste gets questioned and if you buy a large mirror perfect for over the mantel, copper and hammered with bright nails, he seems hurt and refuses to hang it or just lets the moment pass until it has been sitting in your closet for months and doesn't listen to what you have to say about it then or ever.

But on the trip, my friend says, she cared what he thought and he cared what she thought and not only about architecture. What I mean is that they choose to ask about what the other one thinks and then they ask pointed questions about what you think and then they talk about it. *He was a jewel*, she tells me more times than she tells me about the Carpaccio and the martyrdom of Saint Ursula. *You'll like him so much*, she says and arranges for us to meet for dinner and she hangs on him and chooses that moment to lift her left foot so that she needs his arm for balance, and says how charming he is right there in front of him and makes it seem as if no one else is charming and no one has ever done what she's done before.

What does it mean to be so agog about another person who ought to be just furniture, what I mean is, ought to blend in so to speak, not to be tended to but taken for granted, like your brown sofa you don't much notice until a stray cat from the neighborhood gets in and scratches it to bits and you realize now that you see it that you don't like it much, thank goodness since it is ruined.

Do I e-mail her back and tell her it's no good displaying someone else for the world or expecting the world to sit up and take notice of someone as if that someone were not just a man one has chosen for oneself, but a bona fide phenomenon. Perfection is overrated really even if the person does have perfect taste, you feel a bit shoved in the corner, you know, like when I'd chosen the bathroom sconces myself and they did seem right to me at the time. Maybe it's better not to speak about one's choices over and over but just to let them be, the choices one has made, I mean, and get on with it. Like my not choosing anything really for some time now or trying not to, although how one can try not to choose isn't clear to me and isn't something I'd quite thought of until now.

Of course I don't write saying all this to her, any more than I tell her that she needs please to stop talking to me as if I were a child, selfish and unable to accommodate anyone or stand any sort of change, since of course she needs to talk to me this way and who cares really except for thinking about why someone younger would talk to someone older in this way which of course I know the answer already and find it mildly annoying but not so much as to do anything about it.

I mean what can you do when someone thinks they know it all and have made a perfect choice. Although you may be thinking about how I need advice when I go about carelessly dropping everything in the garage and all and how I let the cat get in and why were my doors wide open in the first place and I deserve to have a ruined sofa.

But what I do wonder about and can't stop thinking about is the embracing of another, the human dimension of it, you know, and on the other hand, the arbitrariness of choice which alters everything completely. But then, I don't like living with anyone, can't imagine why anyone would take it on and can't understand why anyone would do it, much less rave on about it. I'm thinking of the nature of willpower, how much some people have and how different it is just thinking about it without having to get up from this sofa which I guess I like well enough after all just as it is, back where it was, even the cat which appears at my feet from time to time having got here from who knows where and seems to have decided, if cats can do such things, to stay.

Cones

It was as light as wind skimming over the surface of the earth, as light as footprints making no mark, a rain that made nothing wet, as if nothing had ever been there, nothing had happened or if it had, had disappeared without a trace, everything erased but for the giant shadow of a cone superimposed on the landscape of a drawing someone had made in soft pencil.

This is the way she was thinking as she was driving the car. And then she thought she wanted to shake him, to wake him up as if he'd gone off to sleep, not that he actually slept more hours, in fact fewer than she did, but that he was of a weight, a sleepiness, possessed it in his being, in his genes as some might say, turned that ring around on his finger in slow motion, and wouldn't tell where it came from or why—given his addiction to the minimal and the strict rules he followed—he consented to wearing jewelry at all. It stood out against his olive skin.

Her mother used to shake her by the shoulders, though not to wake her up, more to bring her down, to calm her, to get her to stop from running in circles, though why she thought shaking would do the trick, she never knew. Afterwards, when she was especially agitated, she thought about it, wished for it, though of course—she pleaded with her memory to yield up its secrets—she never could have been thrown against a wall, too big of course, and no one does such things, and she couldn't remember even being pushed against a wall or against anything else for that matter, though she did remember being shaken, and she would like to shake him to get him to attend, although since he was excruciatingly attentive to certain things, she wasn't sure what she wanted him to attend to.

It was an affair of storms and calms, one that was longer than either had expected and over before anyone would have, if asked, predicted. Which isn't to say that she didn't make extravagant gestures which unnerved him, and which they both knew unnerved him. You must have *Don Giovanni*, she exclaimed. No one exclaims any longer, but she did, rushed out and bought it, forced it upon him and turned it up loud. It filled the room with clashing and passion. He was suspicious, wary of extravagance and made her take it away. She rushed at him. He backed away and she rushed.

She rushed through the market when what he wanted, though not as an articulated desire, but more as a neutral fact, was to touch the world lightly, to disturb

Cones

things less than anyone could imagine possible. He sliced his bread thinner each day and it had to be carefully handled not to tear at the center as he moved it to the toaster; if the butter was too hard, it broke the toast. But he was careful. He had fewer clothes than anyone she'd ever known. It wasn't just that he made do or that he couldn't have bought some few more, although he did have to "watch his pennies" as her father had used to say, but that his pleasures came from having a drawer with four t-shirts, washed out, folded and set one on top of the other. He was especially pleased if they were all the same, all white or all gray or that color they became after many washings, and she thought he ironed them, they were so perfectly flat, or perhaps it was a way of folding she never had time for.

When they went to the market together, she watched him walk the aisles as if he had all the time in the world, had no place to get to, wasn't hungry, didn't much care what he bought. Her trips were always "catch-as-catch-can" between work and home, one thing and another, always some gathering of items in a rush, unbalanced in her arms, the same over and over, but his walking—and it was walking in a way she'd never thought of before—as if what one did in a supermarket wasn't wheel or race, but walk in a desultory and appreciative way. He never bought more than four or five things, whatever he needed for a day or two, but he took so long at it and spent so much extra time at the magazine rack looking over all the new magazines, especially the ones on architecture and houses, that it made her jumpy, unable to stand the neon, the deliberations, the sense that there was all the time in the world. He never bought a magazine, or when he did it was only after having thought about it for several days, returning to get it, not buying it on the spot, but thinking it over. You never think anything over, he said to her; you just grab at things.

She wondered if he thought she grabbed at him. Did he feel she put her hands on him too often and she began to watch herself do it, and watch his movements towards, or, she thought more often, away. She tried to stop, but it was something she simply did as she came through the room and she had a hard time remembering to stop until it was so hard she did. She remembered to sit across from him and keep her arms at her sides. She remembered not to force her cold hands under his arm where she knew it would be warm and not to lop her leg over his just because she felt like it. And in bed she did what she realized belatedly pleased him most; she chose one posture and moved as little as possible. It was not easy or natural, indeed it was as unnatural as she could have imagined, but she thought with great effort of being like a sheet, flat and folded in a drawer; she thought of how he was aroused at her stillness and she managed because it was so arousing itself to find him in her power in this unexpected way.

It was an affair based on the weather. They settled on it and agreed. He liked talking about the weather.

Cones

It came to be for her a gesture like lying still. It was an announcement of how long they had to hold off and of what was to come. For him it was the repetition of a lost childhood, lost porches and Midwestern storms, a past that was most vivid because it had faded like old photographs. He imitated the voice of his grandfather who spoke of what the wind would do or the rain. Since they now lived in Los Angeles, these discussions, like their affair, were attenuated. There wasn't much in the way of weather, or rather, there wasn't much weather for them, for they had come out of the Midwest, and so what happened in the city, small increments of change, had to be sought out, obsessed over, admired and repeated. It wasn't like the snowstorm that overtook her window when she was eleven and it wasn't like the pelting of rain that for months hammered the tin roof and made her think she would go mad if someone didn't come and rescue her from the rain, her parents, her fretful desires.

As a topic, weather is so noncommittal and passes the time so lightly that when they sat waiting for the waiter to arrive at their table, they returned to it regularly. It allowed them to avoid talking about anything too personal and yet to feel, deluded or not, that they were intimately connected because they could go on together about an agreed-upon subject for so long, with so many variations and embellishments, and so they continued on in a quite accomplished pattern about the shifts in humidity, conversations which worked best in May or early June when there was some shift. It allowed them to avoid the extreme vehemence she was prone to. Also the minimal changes in the city's weather allowed them vast tunnels into the past which they both remembered with a fondness bordering on the fanatic or perhaps, since for neither had the present yielded up a life they could recognize, a substitution in some way. In Ohio neither would have fit in; neither would have been at home there now, and indeed she suspected that neither had been other than a misfit even then, but it was a place that together they created as normal, as home, as a place where they might, were things different, have made a life together.

His focus was on the condensation of that odd white light before the rain, the way in which trees came to be defined by that light, harsh almost as neon over the Laundromat, greenish and pale. He remembered a porch and sat himself there time and again, and when he was feeling especially generous, he put her there as well and gave her a tall glass of lemonade with ice cubes. After her initial extravagances, they agreed never to give one another anything other than these memories, these scenic *postcards* embroidered with memories that were more than what they actually remembered. On her birthday, however, he gave her a drawing he had made of a place he agreed they had both visited at one time or other during their childhoods. *The world's going to explode*, he said. The black cones he'd drawn, super-imposed in ink across the picture, were proof.

Cones

He remembered the sounds of birds just before the storm hit. Not only that the light turned itself up a notch. The bird calls intensified and the silvery falling notes of the bird whose name neither of them remembered, only the sound, as if even that link, a name, were unimportant, less important than the thrill of remembering a sound as they both insisted that they did, staring into the space over the table. *Do you remember*, he'd say and she'd settle in.

Sometimes she wanted that porch more than anything, more than their sexual encounters, always so quiet, so without sound or movement, and always she thought, not really the point of whatever they were up to, though what it was they were up to she couldn't say anymore than she could stop. She thought the porch was screened in, everything looked out through a mesh of screen and as the conversation went on, the mesh closed up and darkened and she felt as if she were about to sleep and sleep in some easy way she hadn't slept for years. She remembered the house as well, gray-green and massive with the porch running all around three sides. In the back was a small garden with beans mostly and leaves with red veins running through. Beets buried in the ground. She had no idea where this house was. She knew she'd seen it and she remembered coming around the left side, but whose it was and in what Ohio town, she didn't know. It was a vivid memory that could more easily have belonged to someone else. She focused on his hands. They stood out as in portraits of

Civil War soldiers; they hung down and she could only watch them when he was so involved in his own story, he didn't notice she was staring.

He began. *It dampens one's spirits*, he said, *it comes long and pale, willow leaves across the plains. It's inserted behind every leaf of every tree. It's something like the shape of a hand though not exactly, and one can only watch and so one watches all afternoon. Sitting on the porch all afternoon, the light shifts from white to green to a pulsing absence of all color and I watched the coming light as if my limbs had turned into whatever waiting is. As if by waiting, I had become both absolute distrust and absolute certitude. And then the storm came, cool and breaking over the distance and then right at my feet, and I sat under cover of the porch and stared at the rain coming straight down and taking all the layers off my skin that had gathered all afternoon.*

She was fixed in his description though she didn't know why she could listen to him in that way. Others she knew told stories that were cleverer. It had happened to her throughout her life, someone would be talking and a sort of trance would start to come, to move across her like a coming storm. Sometimes she shook it off, worried that someone would look at her and see how her skin pulled. It was the sound of a voice, his voice, as if the air were heavy and filled with insects, as if something were not about to happen, but just over and done with, and you could contemplate it full and on all sides as a three-dimensional object that floated in the space just in front of where you couldn't take your eyes off it if you wanted.

Cones

He began to give things away. At first she didn't notice. Busy and with a project at work, busy with some semblance of regular life, she didn't notice the small things. But then, one Saturday when she spent the afternoon there, she saw that the corner cabinet was missing. What she noticed first was that the paint on the wall was less faded and then she saw the cabinet that had belonged to his grandparents—he'd told her where it had stood in their house, how he had brought it west and refinished it—was missing. All that was left was a cone of less faded paint. She made tea.

Other things were gone. When he went to the corner for milk, she opened a cupboard with only two cups although he'd always had a collection of mismatched cups, some beautiful if chipped, of a sort of old-fashioned elegance and thinness around which he'd spun stories that she was never sure were true about relatives and long afternoons. Now they were missing. She wondered what to say to him when he returned, pouring milk into the tea, and settling in to some reminiscence or other. She began and then stopped. She was after something more urgently than she could understand, but he was staring at her with the sort of intense blandness that sometimes accompanied their afternoons after bed, so she stopped.

She looked at the corner where the cabinet had been and saw the splatter paintings over screens she had done in grade school, with a toothbrush, a bit of screen in a frame, and a maple leaf. Once the leaf was lifted up, the white left on the page, the image of the leaf itself which was now damp and blue and curled, was pure white and somehow more than the limp thing she held between her fingers. The teacher sent them out to gather leaves in the fall so that on darkening afternoons they could do projects. She shook herself, she gathered what she could of her sense of purpose, she said she'd see him later and he smiled at her blankly. She thought he wanted her to stay or go, either, but not to disturb the air as she moved.

He gave away his old tape player. *Where is it*, she began and then stopped. *Why did you give it away? It was broken*, he said, though she knew that a week ago it hadn't been broken, that they had sat in the fading light for two hours and listened to the Bach unaccompanied cello, and he told her he'd never had that tape, she was welcome to look, but when she did, it wasn't there.

And then he left the apartment and walked towards the bus stop and she was standing by her car wondering where he was going. He had a box of books under his arm. The books had begun to disappear as well and she wondered as she drove home if he were moving, and where was he moving and why she couldn't ask. Most of his books came from the library; he was one of the few she knew who used the library, but he had some few paperbacks, many smelling of foxing and paper dust. She liked going through the box he had under the bed.

Cones

He liked, she thought, to have her for an audience, going through the same photographs again and again of his young mother, his grandmother, and the picture of the porch with the snowball bush to the side. He could pass his thumb and fingers over these for hours and talk about the way he'd seen the storms coming, the exact weather in August, the ways people talked in those days. His stories varied little. She liked the sameness, the return to the same descriptions, the shaping of the shadow against the wall, the planks of the floorboards, the eyes of the knots in the wood.

Why then did she feel like shaking him, as if he were in a state of sleep? Why then did she feel she'd entered a realm in which photographs lied? He hadn't ever been on that porch, he'd bought them with his old cups and his old books at a flea market, the family was someone else's altogether. Perhaps the photographs had been picked at random from some junk store, perhaps that woman in the flowered dress on the porch had no connection to him whatsoever and perhaps he's never been on the porch at all. *Would you like more tea*, he asked politely.

She could feel the trance coming on. It was a cloud of dew, faded and in faded color. He was telling her about a place he wanted to visit. It was Kyoto he said, and he began to show her photographs of gardens, gardens with raked stone, one garden with a giant white cone in the center. *The world is coming to an end*, he said. *I have to visit Japan before it happens.* Was he joking, she wondered? He had barely enough money for rent and food and yet he was as serious as she'd ever seen him. In the corner of the room he had put three stones, a start of something perhaps. He said gardeners pull up every weed, every bit of green, creating a calm ocean of stillness, a replica of ripples just barely indented across the graveled surface. He turned the pages slowly and forced her to focus on the photograph. The book itself was tiny, a small edition meant to be carried in a pocket, so small that it was impossible to flatten the pages and almost impossible for more than one person to look at unless they moved awkwardly close together. His hand looked outsized; it was large in any case and always looked larger, she thought, because his arms were thin and long. She stared at the veins on his left hand, at the veins in the maple leaf, at the tiny book. It had never occurred to her to want to go anywhere, much less to a place as foreign and far off as Japan; it was so at odds with what she thought of as their history and she thought he had thought this too. Wasn't he the one who was nostalgic, the one who talked on and on about that quite ordinary porch and the patch that produced summer squash and corn. What had these cold white arrangements to do with that, she thought, and found herself sunken and irritated.

One day he burned the last book on the grate. She saw the cone of ashes, fragile and insistent and unswept. Next time the bed was gone. He was sleeping, he said, on a sort of bedroll, like being in the army. When were you ever in the army, she asked. He made them tea, but this time it was green and bitter and she couldn't drink it, and he presented it to her as if he were moving in slow motion. And there was only one cup. He wanted to share it with her, insisted on his taking a sip followed by her taking a sip, but she didn't want this tea he offered and the handle had been snapped off and she could only stare at the jagged spot.

At the edge of the parking lot to the market there was a man wrapped in a dirty blanket. She saw how brown his skin was from sleeping in the sun. She got some groceries and parked at the far end of the parking lot before going home. The ice cream melted through the brown paper bag and left a triangular stain on the seat. She couldn't stop thinking about the roll of a man and about what she should do.

After a few weeks passed in which she had stayed away on purpose, she found herself thinking of black and white cones, of sand and stone and shapes, and it was all she could think of. Had he learned, she wondered, to fire a gun, and had he really been in the army? Why would the world come to an end just now and why would he think so? She thought about how easily things passed away. If she didn't see him, perhaps these thoughts would go away; she thought maybe if she just didn't see him or if she stopped putting her thumb into the slight indentation on the way up the stairs. I've stopped, she told herself. I'll never do it again. It's the same thing, however, she knew, it was the same always to do something or always not to do it. She didn't go back. Sometimes she'd ask a casual question of someone, but no one ever responded in a way particular enough to let her know.

She decided to paint her living room and moved all the furniture into the middle and covered it all with old sheets so that the room was transformed into a figure of sorts, one draped chair positioned against another. She bought paint and looked at everything rearranged. In the corner the original paint was still bright, and from the wall emerged a shape she was startled to recognize.

The Tattoo

First he had faces done in the crook of his elbow, small elegant faces with hooked noses and flat cheekbones. Then, overlaid across the top of the faces, came zigzag designs as if the faces were peering out from behind ornate screens or trying to escape the foliage of interlocking vines, the loopy arrangement of what looked to be organic, intestinal. Each time he went back the faces were more obscured, and yet perhaps because they were so hard to make out, they took on a kind of salience so that although at first it had been possible to take them, if not for granted, but just to take them, afterwards they seemed to announce something. Why didn't he take on some other area of his body she wondered, why did he keep returning to the same right arm, fingers even, like a person who knows it's time to move, but keeps on in the same apartment piling up books and knowing it is time to move someplace bigger where the neighbors don't scream that they'll pull their kids' arms out of their sockets. She counted the layers of tattoos across his right arm, like a filmy layer that could be lifted off like Chinese paper cutouts in a shop she'd found, flimsy, delicate, concise. He wore only long-sleeved button-down shirts, blue, the left sleeve rolled down and buttoned at the wrist, always a bit short on his long arm, the other rolled up high exposing the tattoos, the whole thing extremely and properly contrived.

He wrote letters in longhand, precise cursive script, the sort practiced in elementary school. He left notes around, each one done in that perfect hard pressed ballpoint script that went through to layers beneath, leaving a message pressed into the yellow pad after the top layer had been torn off and crumpled. He left a note on the box of coffee filters: *Use two*. And on the coffee cup: *Soak in bleach*. And on the front table: *I've gone for a few days*. She studied the curves of the letters for clues, but was unable to detect anything definitive and when he returned she didn't ask. She didn't know why; it simply seemed intrusive and against some set of rules she thought might be in place, so she opted for the elegance of silence. He asked if she had soaked the cups.

You go on for such a long time when nothing happens, nothing out of the ordinary, so you assume it will go on for quite a long time, not forever, no one thinks forever, but for quite a long time. And then things clump together freakishly: your dog dies, you have an accident coming out of the car wash and your wrist doesn't heal, your friend turns spidery thin, thinner than you could have imagined and her hair falls out like your mother's before she died, and you're caught in a pocket of turbulence you can't seem to get out of. You know it won't go on forever, but you can't get it out of your voice on the phone, that edge is there even when you try to relax and breathe and everyone has long since stopped noting it. It becomes a usual hitch, a usual way people think of you.

You are startled that ordinary ventures that once seemed so ordinary even in the days when you were trying to be hypersensitive, turn out to be trials for you. Now you have to be pushed onto the road to go where you'd planned to go in the first place and talk to your heart to keep it from pounding in your mouth. You breathe into a paper bag. Someone tells you to try acupuncture—it made her want to rush right out and eat a steak she says—and so you try it and drive to the corner afterwards and can't remember whether to turn right or left, and although you have the directions written out, you can't seem to reverse left and right in order to get back on track and you feel limp, unable to get a breath, and you can't imagine, although she had insisted it was true, that she'd been positively ravenous.

———

Watching him, she thought to say, you duck your head as if you're being cuffed, and wondered why she thought of cuffed and the kids who'd lived next door whose father said, do that again and I'll pull your arms out of your sockets. From the top floor of the apartment she could look down into their back bit of yard by the garage. Four or five children, hair wispy and thin, were there playing with sticks, a small matchbox truck, a broom. One rode around and around on the broom shouting something she couldn't hear. One nursed a doll, its hair brushed back from its forehead again and again in meaningless repetition, hay-like stuff. It refused to lie flat. She looked across the room at him. His head jerked to the side when he was concentrating on something or when he sat to write. He wants someone to hit him, she thought.

It's the overlap that gets you, that you can't stop thinking about. You are in one place but you know that in a few days or even, and this happens quite often, a few hours, you will be standing someplace else and you can smell the airport or the pissy metallic air of the train and although you try to hang onto where you are and look at the tree outside the window, anchored there, or you fold up napkins in smaller and smaller squares, you can't help being in one of those dislocations that is so ordinary, not preposterous at all, and therefore eminently dismissible, and you find yourself queasy. You keep saying: knock against something, push over a chair, crack your knuckles on the door. But you see yourself going under the arch at the airport security where sometimes someone sets it off, and you are there looking at their keys in the tray or at the camera. Someone keeps asking will the film be OK, and someone has always bought something at Macy's, a large red towel stuffed into a paper shopping bag that is already tearing at the edges, although he has just started his trip home, and you wonder why he bought a towel on his vacation when you can get a towel anywhere, and it gets caught against another suitcase on the ramp and he is tying it up with a small rope he has in his left pocket, and you wonder how he knew to bring a small rope for tying up a bag that hadn't ripped when he started out.

⸺

He's gone back for more tattoos. He keeps getting them on the same arm and hand and perhaps, although she can't quite see underneath the roll of his oxford cloth shirt, the designs go up and up even to his shoulder and over the crest of his shoulder and onto his back. She can't help wondering where they go and when they will stop. He has a friend who does them at cut rate so it doesn't cost him so much and he can discuss what sorts at great length and so they spend hours at it. Most are of pre-Columbian design. He wants to have a collection of precious and previously owned pottery, but he settles for making himself a sort of collectable, a piece of what he would wish to own. He's got all sorts of books to authenticate the designs and he keeps adding to his collection of books and to the lines in color across his arm that don't, as tattoos often do, announce anything, but rather keep the message hidden in abstraction. No "mother" or "J" or even rippling snakes. His are rare, overlapped, elaborate. She keeps thinking it must be excruciating to have a needle go in and out, in and out, stitching the skin of one's own body, but he doesn't let her go with him and watch. When he catches her staring at his arm, he turns on the TV and sits against the chair at an angle to blot her out and she washes dishes more carefully then and uses bleach with an old toothbrush on the tile.

One day when she returned she found the set of steak knives someone had given her as a birthday present missing, the entire set unused and resting side by side like Egyptian mummies, missing. It was the only thing she couldn't locate; she checked around and although she didn't have much of value, there were things a thief might have taken and her jewelry, easily accessible in a wooden box on top of the dresser, was still there. Only later in the week when she happened to look down on the lot next door did she see the kids carving x's and o's in the caked dirt with the knives, making elaborate roadways for the truck, printing out letters sometimes forwards and sometimes backwards as children do. The girl was sitting apart with the doll, sawing on an arm. They didn't seem to be after each other as one might have anticipated, but moved in a hungry slow sort of motion, focused only on that small ring of a world they lived in.

— ∾ —

Your hands grow dry from the Clorox and cleaning. You buy rubber gloves but forget to put them on. You were warned your skin would grow dry and scaly and you always try to remember, but you are in the middle of something before you remember, sprinting into it before you think of where you are going and by then it is too late. You are soaking the cups, you are scrubbing in between kitchen tiles, tiles too old and stained ever to come clean no matter how much time is spent scrubbing late into the night but when you can't sleep that's when it's good to get up and do something, to change things, if only the smell of things. It's like being asleep anyhow, over and over, and afterwards you sleep, if you're lucky, the sleep of the blessed, quiet, still, wrapped up tight in a summer sheet. It's only later you begin to worry at your cuticles, tearing at the dry bits of skin for the ache of relief.

He'd bought one small rug and it too had zigzags across it, like his arm, his favorite sweater, his guinea hen, stuffed and dusty and on the shelf she wasn't supposed to notice; who'd given him such a thing and why had he carried it about, this child's toy, for so many years. When the yarn unraveled at the cuff of the sweater, it took on that same zigzag pattern, that repetition she locked on to. She saw the sweater hanging on a hook in the front hall where she'd painted the floorboards white, deck white; the salesman at the hardware warned her but she wanted to bring in light and order, to remake the dirty and scuffed floor in the image of a deck beneath a deck chair that would look out over the sea and away. Now it was, as the salesman had said it would be, smudged and dirty, though surreptitiously and late at night she wet it down with the corner of a rag, hooked over a forefinger, the small sections in front of the coat rack, clean and slippery, pale as an egg.

The face on his arm was contorted either with pleasure or pain, something occurring somewhere deep in its anatomy, off-screen, off the arm, out of the frame. The teeth of St. Sebastian, the pearly white drops of Mantegna's Sebastian, eyes raised and arrows through the skin and into the groin, those unexpected doll-like teeth between slightly parted lips. They looked fake like bits of tile, painted and varnished and polished. This was not a smile, clearly not. Some piece of anatomy was out of range, was being pulled or stretched or pierced and she sometimes wished the entire face would disappear in a tangle of lines and bloody dots so she wouldn't have to think anymore.

She wondered when it would all end. The Thai restaurant she used to go to had been turned into a tattoo parlor; the woman who sold pliers and screws at the hardware store had butterflies all over her arm; the man at the video store pulled up his shirt to show her. She knew it would all heal soon, she'd seen it before. She'd read a story about a Japanese tattooer who fell madly in love with the ankle of a woman who passed in a flash past the door of his shop and for years he waited for her to return and when she did he drugged her and tattooed an enormous spider across her smooth white back.

The Tattoo

She felt evaporated like a line of paper dolls, not just one body flattened and about to go up in smoke, but a whole line of them. She had made such dolls as a child and had always begged her mother to burn them at the end of the day. She'd sit in front of the fire and watch them curl up and turn brown at the edges of their skirts and then disappear. Her mother wanted her to keep them in a box or wait to show them off, but she wasn't interested in anything but the making and unmaking, the pleasure of a long line of intricate and identical dolls, gone. She began with the sorts of scissors made for children, clumsy and with rubberized handles, graduated to her mother's sewing scissors, and one Christmas was given a small pair of scissors in the shape of a bird. Finally, however, she had to use nail scissors, the tiniest of nail scissors to get the proper angles and proportions. The best cutouts had hair that stuck in peaks and looked thin and frayed; they lay there across the log tranquil and white, waiting for the match. It was and remained the most exquisite of moments, finally calm.

He began to write more notes for her than before, many more notes, but then they were mysteriously missing. He wrote and wrote late into the night, but then, for reasons she didn't understand, he took them away with him when he left in the morning, both shirt sleeves down and buttoned. On the paper pads left scattered through the apartment were, however, the pressings and indentations of his ballpoint, the short ones she could fairly easily make out—soak the coffee

cups or remember to buy coffee—but longer ones about
some book he'd been reading, notes on the conquest of
America or the practices of the Mayans, in which she
could almost make out quotations. The impress was so
strong and the pads so obviously placed for her to find,
she knew she was supposed to know some version of a
pleasure. If I match the markings with the books, she
thought, if I find the quotation in a book, I'll be able to
read it there, if I can only match the swirls and curves,
which she couldn't.

*The text of the altar, carved on top around the edge,
is eroded. It has been impossible to restore the carved
stela to its original condition, as many fragments are
missing. It is suspected that Postclassic peoples tam-
pered with the shattered stela, or may even have broken it themselves. Although it is clear that the figure
turned to the frontal position, naked but for loincloth
and ornate slippers, is human, and that the profile is
that of a jaguar, it is impossible to know whether it is
a human dressed to be the jaguar, or the jaguar taking on human guise.*

Something else changed. He adopted a new and,
she found, quite disconcerting habit. Instead of hiding
when she stared at his arm, he made himself available.
He draped his arm across the arm of a chair, unbuttoned
his blue shirts, so that his chest showed, hollow, white,
his arm open to full view. Instead of having to work to

74

see the new designs, she found them put on display: curlicues and more bands with red and black flecks, faces caught in the filigree of leaves, hair that snaked across foreheads and lines that broke and joined and broke again. She could hardly stand to walk into the room where he sat, could hardly stand the blare of his arm. Animals she couldn't recognize bared their teeth, beaks clamped, headdresses coiled and feathered into the air. You look as if you want someone to burn you up, throw you out. You look as if you want to be thrown against the wall.

She sat down to read the newspaper. When she couldn't look any longer at the jumble of *e*'s and *o*'s and *m*'s in front of her, a story she thought about a recent plane crash, although she couldn't be sure, and thought, you have to have your eyes checked, yes, that's what you ought to do and she thought to write it down so she wouldn't forget, but felt herself drawn into the other room where he sat, moving his arm out along the chair, and as she watched it seemed to get longer, seemed to extend beyond the wooden knob at the end of the overstuffed chair and out into the room. It was almost black with design, almost completely filled in as if his purpose had been almost fulfilled, and he were finally content. And she too felt a sort of heavy contentment like a mantel of feathers come over her shoulders and down her back. It could have been a tangled mat of black hair coating his arm, so thick the lines had become and would feel fuzzy like hair, the skin broken and healed over, lines turned to hair. She felt for the raw edge of her thumb, the broken and raw cuticle, moving forefinger over thumb again and again. She felt her face burn and was sure that without moving and without lifting his hand into the air which was so smoky and thick to burn her eyes and make her blink back the watering, making it more and more difficult to keep the healing lines in any semblance of focus, he would hit her flat across the left side of her face, a clear ancient profile against the white of the wall.

Her Subject/His Subject

When I raise my arm I do not usually try to raise it (Wenn ich meinen Arm hebe, versuche ich meistens nichts, ihn zu heben).
—Wittgenstein

Her subject is people in landscapes of estrangement; his subject is the landscape. *You are never looking out the window,* he says to her. *Here you are driving through the most beautiful section of the California coast, and you are talking to me about a novel you are reading, the words on the pages, the characters' clothes. I am in the scotch broom,* he says, and yes, he seems to be as far as I can tell, and he is right I am not. It is everywhere on the side of the hill wherever the redwoods take a break and one ought to smell its sweet smell but all I can smell is eucalyptus and that's what grows by my bedroom window at home.

We drive for hours. He thinks about the fog blowing in off the ocean. It drifts over the fields and over the road. One moment we can't see the road, the next it is clear. Sometimes he is talking about his subject and sometimes not, but it is always what's there. When we stop at a rest stop and look out over the view he knows how the gullies were formed, what the weather patterns will be, which ridges connect north and south.

To me the foggy blur over the tops of trees is a mental affair. You hold in your mind another time and live there in that other imagined time while the present time, new and raw in some way, presses for attention. But the other time is held like a fragile glass, transparent but up close in front of one's face. This is a practice from childhood. It serves no purpose except to counter the insistence of present time and to block it a bit. I can't remember when I haven't done this. Being in two places at one time. This is my definition of a person, I say, as if I were saying something definitive and true. He thinks I'm trying to be clever.

It began, no doubt, as a protective device. That seems to make sense. But when you try to think of when it was that the other time became important, you can't. It ought to have been a sharp pain that wrenched one time from another, made you opt out for good reason, but you can't think of one. You can think of a year when you fell from the rotted tree in the side yard and broke your arm but the pain is merely a word, not even as vivid as the small scar. And anyhow, what would it be to think of a sharp pain which is not something most of us can do. All I can think of is someone large leaning over my hunched shoulders telling me to try, *try* she said, *to sit still*. The racing part of my body was still racing out the back door, into the backyard, and out into the street where it had been just moments before and I was trying. The idea of trying is what puts one in two places at once since the idea of trying also contains the idea of not trying. I want to try, I want to know how to say to her in that time so long ago, but I have no way to think about what I am thinking and so I don't.

He doesn't have to try to drive, but I do. I guess he is paying attention all right, but he isn't trying. When I drive I have to try hard to pay attention, to keep to the road, to follow directions, to fend off the fear of getting lost. Nothing seems so bad as that fear of turning the wrong way or finding oneself broken down on the country road with only a dim light from a distant farmhouse. I am surrounded by darkness. I try to keep calm. I try to remind myself way ahead of time to keep calm if anything should happen. I get tired of trying even when everything goes smoothly and I clutch the steering wheel. Here I am, I say to myself, trying to get myself to watch the view as if it were an unnatural act, even though, one would suppose, it is the most natural thing in the world. Look at all those people doing it, I say to myself; surely you too can look out the window at the view. You too can admire the scenery. His subject, the landscape. Try it.

———

But even the ringing in her ears takes her away and even the effort of sitting still in the car for so long, even the book she tries to forget. Her novel is a novel in which the narrator becomes someone else momentarily. She loses herself in imagining herself a child and she imagines this so strongly that she begins to blurt things out, slurp the milk out of her cereal bowl, race in circles among the trees stomping in pools of shallow water. She makes no attempt to conform to the rules, this child, but neither does she break them; she simply moves through the world and does what comes to mind. What comes to mind is rather sing-songy and windy, hooting softly, gazing out and running far. The child stands in the side yard by the rotted tree. She takes off her red sweater and makes a cape. She fixes the buckle on her red shoe. She stares for hours at the view. Although she doesn't at that time live anywhere near what one might call a view, no vistas or California coastlines, it doesn't matter to her. She stands at the side of the road and looks down it. She doesn't move. She sees a rock and she sees it up close for a long time. Her mother calls for her but she doesn't come, not because she is trying to disobey, but because it just doesn't occur to her to come.

Years later she sees an elaborately constructed miniature garden planted into the cleft of a great stone, the tiniest rock garden she's ever seen with lichen, alpine plants of various sorts, saxifrages, gentians, pinks, penstemons and what looks to be a fold with a red dot in the center. The novel isn't a great novel, perhaps it hasn't yet been written, but it is what she is thinking about when he says again, look at the view and there are waves crashing against the boulders and melting down into waterfalls and crashing again. It is almost larger than she can stand and she's back at the restaurant looking through her water glass. Through the crash of the waves, she thinks she hears him asking something.

The Gift

The two are perfect lovers because neither can focus or is interested in focusing. What each likes best as it becomes obvious to them both is the neutrality each is able to effect after a sexual encounter—each of which is necessarily quickly and almost matter-of-factly executed, *more* for each of them by the very fact of its being *less*, more pleasurable as it approaches the experience of simply the drinking of a coffee at a café, sipping a glass of peach iced tea against the heat of August. Thus it is not, as one might expect in the heat of summer in Italy, the sexual liaison which binds them so tightly, but rather the hours of nonchalance afterwards, the pretense that is so perfected as to call absolutely no attention to itself, to be banal and, occasionally and at its best, even slipshod.

Perhaps the story begins with Paola, the woman. Perhaps with the man, an American in charge of the language program and having an affair with Paola, the director of the college in Bologna which houses the program, an affair that cannot—fortunately they agree—be acknowledged even by the two of them even in private, in part because such acknowledgment might change their behavior in small but perceptible ways, and in part because to acknowledge it would be a confession that one's body is not ruled by one's mind. Or perhaps it all begins with the narrator herself who might describe herself as attentive and agile, but also a bit out of her element, having just and somewhat awkwardly arrived from the States on invitation, an invitation that turns out to have been issued prematurely, from the man.

To begin with, Paola is trying to attain a more prestigious position as Cultural Affairs Director in the local government and since her boyfriend, a minor but influential politician, can help her to this position, he must be kept in the dark. Indeed neither of the lovers is willing to be fully cognizant of the affair, not only because of political complications, but more importantly for reasons which have to do with temperaments which in this case are similar in an uncanny way, as when one finds a match to a plate one already owns in a junk store in a distant and entirely other corner of the globe, a match which provides its own vivid if not especially significant pleasure.

They always have, the narrator surmises, so much to attend to with the students, one of whom tries to commit suicide ineffectively and theatrically. Indeed, all of the theatricality of the lovers is transposed onto

the students and they—Paola and the man—tell endless
stories of the students' sexual adventures, *their* hysteri-
cal reactions, *their* betrayals—not to contain their own
and certainly not as substitute, but as simple fact. It is
not that their many meals together, cooked for themselves, students, friends and other colleagues, are a
means to spend more time together; rather, they are
part simply of the ordinary unfolding of a day in summer in Italy—what anyone would expect. Nor do they
glance at one another longingly across the room while
they serve wine or pasta—such would be shabby and
beneath them—rather, they are fully *in* the event as it
is, not in coy relation to it, not wishing to be elsewhere,
not living with the pressure of time and an imagined
next encounter.

They exchange no symbolic gestures, no bits of paper, no gifts. His having brought her a knife for cooking
is only a knife for cooking since he must prepare food
for the guests, since her kitchen was without one, since
it is a practical thing and, moreover, since it is only a
mildly generous gesture, not excessive or out-of-keeping.
If anyone were to point to the obvious symbolism, they
would scoff and be embarrassed, not for themselves, but
for the person who would think such an obvious thought.
The absence of such thinking is what binds them. The
power of ideology is what makes it possible for them to
turn from the metaphysical and sentimental in a manner
which implies neglectful lassitude, no matter the depth
of the roots, the tangle of historical precedence. What

these lovers are so adept at is simplification by means of high drama, but always high drama not their own.

Also the man's daughter is visiting and it might be, the narrator once thought wrongly, necessary for pains-taking discretion, but, neither lover has noticed her presence, or rather neither has noticed in any excessive way, although he praises his daughter's adolescent beauty at every opportunity and especially in public when she has gone in to bed for the night. For the daughter's part, she adores him and is always pulling her clothes aside to show her sunburned skin or talking about the reaction to her see-through bathing suit on the beach or insisting on shoes so high-heeled and uncomfortable that her father must call cabs for her to go anywhere, which he believes she is owed because unlike the students he teaches, he insists, she is without wealth or guile. The cabs pay for his guilt.

He is guilty for having left his wife in the States. Although they are psychically estranged and live to-gether guardedly—she having taken up a purportedly secret lover—he knows she has done this in response to his years of neglect and so feels, not guilty—since his leftist ideology leads him to oppose guilt on prin-ciple—but uneasy, although others would think it, he knows, perfectly within his rights to have taken a lover as well. Only he also knows, to his credit perhaps, that their estrangement is not the result of her lover who is simply a lover. He knows that his inattentiveness (not in bed—it hadn't so much to do with that—but with a vaguer and more encompassing inattentiveness that he would will away if he could) has not encouraged her, but has left her open, if not vulnerable, to anyone who might approach her.

One night he was relieved to watch his wife's new lover sit at table and engage her, ask her questions, listen to her not foolish responses (because indeed he allows himself to think no one foolish, especially not his wife whom he finds touching), but to responses that he felt obliged to dismiss, for reasons he couldn't name exactly. Her facts weren't wrong; they were, rather, extravagant—she tended to "enthuse"—and so it was more with relief than jealousy that he watched this lovely man take on his lovely wife as if her gestures were, as he knew they were, beautiful, as if her account of a walk she had taken the night before were, as it indeed was, expressive, if also, so he judged, overly poetic and gushing. He didn't wish to be embarrassed by her lack of verbal restraint, and, indeed, wasn't just one moment later when he found himself still sitting at table, entirely at ease and cheered by the thought of acute angles, infinity, space. He might, he thinks, looking at the lover looking at her, want to behave in exactly this way, if by some stroke of fate he were another person or a person he used to be, perhaps, or if it weren't at odds with his resolve, or more precisely his leaning towards the inattentive, but such lines of thinking he found useless and he cut them into shorter and shorter segments.

The Gift

Sometimes he wondered himself when his wife described the shape of flowers which she loved so well, getting the color of a petal exactly right or the color of their daughter's "faded rose" socks which he himself had folded in the laundry basket (thinking also of how he loved both of these women, the older blond and the girl with the same blond hair), why such description drove him mad, made him want—although he never would do so decidedly crude a thing—an act of violent disruption. At night at home he would get in his car and drive and drive until emptiness defeated her too heady perfume.

Which is why, the narrator thought, his new Italian lover had such a so-much-better chance with him, because she drew him not intellectually exactly, but disembodyingly, not because she was not a physical being, indeed her particular and acrid odor was the very announcement of sexuality, but that she knew how to set it aside for him so that it was impossible for him not to be at her side, not pulled—for that would suggest something too raw, but drawn there nonetheless.

At a local restaurant they sit across from one another at a large table looped over by fellow teachers, resident philosophers and their girlfriends, students and leather jackets. He never looks in her direction although she is speaking in a voice raised just a notch over the din of glasses and conversation so he can be sure to hear her without anyone's attention being drawn to the fact that everything she is saying is directed at him, designed for him, an echo of his phrases and his words of American slang, albeit with a slight but pronounced accent. He sees the narrator looking at her and then at him and he accords her a quizzical if fleeting moment of attention as if he were noting the pressure of her overt attention. Paola laughs easily as if the efforts on his side were only communal and not at all meant, as the narrator is sure they are meant, for her.

He calls her a cultural geisha, his only and always public acknowledgment of her gifts; Paola speaks to him only of office arrangements, train schedules, and the abroad students, knowing that these are the absolute arrows to his heart. What the narrator has to come to try to see is whether their behavior is a philosophical choice or a moral failing. And to whom would it make a difference? Certainly not to the narrator, since it has nothing to do with her, but to anyone? And if the narrator is drawn ever more powerfully to the man, for what reason could it be except to state the obvious, to bring into the open all that is, not hidden from anyone since everyone knows even if no one speaks of it, including the almost totally self-involved student who burns her arms with cigarettes and weeps into the night. So, the question becomes whether the narrator knows that someone will be hurt and who that someone will be. She must come to recognize the crudeness of her own responses, knowing as she does the sexual odor coming off Paola's clothes and squirminess of the men smoking cigars at the back of the café.

The Gift

If the narrator becomes the interpreter of events between the man and the woman, what does that mean except that they have maneuvered her, without lifting a finger, only counting on her pallor and paranoia, into a position that they had not even dared to hope for and have, therefore, a witness which neither one of them is willing to be and which makes their affair not more but less real, for the very unreliability of the witness, and also, somehow, protected.

Like a person without a reflection, each needs another sort of person to be a witness, which is why the narrator is useful to them and perhaps why the affair ultimately fails or is able, depending on the complicity of the narrator and her ability to dampen her own ardor and to become, devotedly, the third point in the triangle, to go on unacknowledged for quite some time.

My Son and the Bicycle Wheel

In 1913 I had the happy idea to fasten a bicycle wheel to a kitchen stool and watch it turn. . . . It was around that time that the word "Readymade" came to mind to designate this form of manifestation. A point which I want very much to establish is that the choice of these "Readymades" was never dictated by aesthetic delectation. This choice was based on a reaction of visual indifference.

—Marcel Duchamp

He said, my son said, you just don't get it, I'm not like you. What does it mean, I'm not like you. I think differently, act differently, move about differently, don't like you, can't stand you and what about the waver in both our voices when we come to this point in the conversation. A street sign: Go Left or None of Your Business. That could be it, I'm asking too many questions as usual and interfering in his life, of course.

You'd get on with them, he says, you're like them, but I don't. I couldn't do it, work there I mean or anything. I can't adopt the pose, manage the portfolio, stand at attention and besides they think I'm weird. You don't see me, but they do and they know I don't fit in. You'd fit in, he says it again, you would, because it's where you went to school and everything, but not me and I don't want to anyhow.

It's a hot day and growing hotter and I hate talking on the telephone when I'm late and it seems I'm always late when he calls with something important to say.

He makes up stories. Sometimes when he's talking I am back in time with his father but I never tell him this because he is, of course, a separate being, but then the only person who reminds me of him is his father telling stories and making me laugh as I never laughed when I was growing up where laughter was a mockery of whatever serious endeavor we were all supposed to be engaged in.

But the stories don't help with *I'm not like you*. What can it mean exactly. It's like an abrupt bend in the road which you don't see and are out over the air in your mind, wheels spinning, heart pounding. Not that you think you are alike since even you can see that you're not. But it's the phrase and what it means beyond the fact that he likes one kind of food and you like another or that he grew up here and you grew up there or that you analyze everything and he thinks it's weird. He's a great cyclist, Cat 2, and has raced in several cities and then smaller ones I've never heard of and he comes in with the pack or wins or trains by riding to the top of

Mt. Wilson which is about 65 miles round trip in a day and comes in and walks to the refrigerator, ravenous and bent over in insect clothes unable to utter a word much less tell a story.

When he was a kid I was a single mom. I thought of course that I could do everything because that's really what one has to think, but as the years unfold, one realizes that one is a paltry number and also that as he reminds you, you live in one world and he in another. He saw a home movie once of me riding a bike decorated with crepe paper in a Fourth of July parade in the middle of Ohio. No wonder he says, and he shakes his head.

So what do we talk about. We talk about the movies which of course is what everyone talks about, although again, he likes movies in which things happen and I like those in which things don't. Who wants anything to happen and I think this more and more; there is too much happening all over anyhow and what we need to do is slow things down.

He races bicycles. Brilliantly as it turns out. When he was five I took him to the nearby park to learn to ride which he didn't want to. I won't he said and he said it again. You will I said. I held the back of the seat and launched him forward until he fell and then launched him again until by the end of the afternoon he could do it. He didn't want to but then he did and then he did every afternoon when I came home from work and before I could put my feet up or listen to my messages, we were at the park and he was riding and jumping over jumps and taking off.

My Son and the Bicycle Wheel

My first memory of sheer joy is riding a bike. It was an adult bike much too big for me and so I had wooden blocks on the pedals which I could push only standing up. It was a year or two before I could ride the bike sitting on the seat but I could ride it much farther then because I could sit down once in a while. He had always been indifferent to my stories of riding, riding without hands, riding the neighborhood, getting away from everyone, riding to outride the boys on the block, riding into the sunset with my cowboy hat flapping against the back of my t-shirt. No wonder he said looking at me as if I were a foreign object he had just suddenly encountered in his living room. But one day he looked at me and said, I've inherited the bicycle gene, I'm just like you. Of course he wasn't, he'd been right in the first place, he wasn't just like me, but it was a good story.

GLASS GRAPES

Myopia

Myopia fosters a sense of possibility one never quite
gets over, quite gives up. One can't quite see. One is allowed another scenario, another way in which things
might turn out, things lost and forgotten. One gets dizzy
enough to pass from one realm to another. As a child I
could fly about the upstairs guest room with its heavy
furniture, its yellow wallpaper, its corner window. I was
to take a nap. My eyes went dim. The ribbons on the
wallpaper swerved and looped. My grandmother had
just died in the spring; at the grave site, it was painfully
cold. In the room I hung in the corner and visited the
window, gazing at the tree which grew just a bit each
year, a bit I could almost see as if in a time-lapse film.
How unfair it seemed when I could no longer do this.
It was an effort I remember as if my skin shrunk tight
over my bones and my brain expanded in my skull, but
it was an effort I could manage until one day I couldn't.
It made my stomach turn somersaults, but it was worth

it and it was better even than the sidewalk glide, better than out-of-focus movies, even though I knew I had to get back under the covers before mother returned, had to feign the ordinary, had to be convincing. Someone might come back from the dead.

In the fifth grade we did reports on time zones, each zone in a different color, and I got so dizzy my eyes dimmed and I was sent to lie down in the nurse's office. How can you stand it, I asked the nurse, all those times at the same time. Everything passing by, disappearing. She stuck a thermometer in my mouth and went out.

Things lying in the street have a magnetism that is so uncanny one swerves the car not only to keep from hitting the dead body of a possum or skunk, but to shut out the idea of what has already happened. I am driving to a 3:00 P.M. appointment. I am swerving away from the dead bodies. I am trying on glasses at the optometrist. I have to get new ones because my others disappeared. I don't tell the assistant that I knew they would disappear. That I had bought the frames at a flea market in London. That Barbara had said I had to—they were cheap and stylish and with blue lenses fitting in I could drift in and out of afternoon pool parties in LA. It would be as if I didn't need corrective lenses, just wanted to see the world through glass-bottle blue. The lights in the garden would blink to each of my steps around the reflecting pool that hung at the edge of the yard at the drop-off, so that it looked as if the silver water went on forever into sky.

I didn't say that I knew they would disappear. They were just gone as I'd predicted and I was caught in that out-of-time experience of trying to reconstruct my movements, hands in and out of a purse, at a restaurant, by the TV, in the freezer where I found the key to the back door. It is a flat key; it rests perfectly flat along the top of the freezer door as if someone had acted both to hide it and to put it in exactly the right place to find it easily, except I have no memory of having put it there.

I didn't tell her that they were the glasses of my childhood, the ones I had to wear in fifth grade, the ones I hated and could see my feet through, a time from the past that came back now full force. I remember the look of the sidewalk as my mother and I exited the doctor's office. The sidewalk came up to meet me. The silver river along which I had walked to school in a dreamy haze was now divided into square cement segments, pock-marked and stained. It was a real sidewalk, which is what, I realized, it had always been. My feet were big and clumsy in brown lace-ups. I wanted to say, take them away, give me the silver river, but I did what was required: I held my mother's hand and said yes when she asked if I liked the pinkish plastic frames she had just picked out.

When I hear the Tokyo String Quartet playing Hindemith, time seems caught in an endless and diz-zying groove. The globe is spinning faster. From the balcony of the auditorium the chandelier is a magnet. Someone's pink face is swinging in the rafters and I

Myopia

almost can make it out. I see the dizzying swing of it, the arc of leaping into the air above the heads of those below, grabbing hold of the crystals, a fistful in each hand, and swinging into the expanding universe.

The Lightbulb

We were sitting on the edge of two twin beds crammed into a tiny road-front room. There was an overhead bulb. He sat on one wooden foot of a bed and I on the one next to it as we talked about our lives and what had happened since we had seen each other. Cars went by on the wet street below us.

Years later I was driving along the same street with a friend who asked why I put up with him. I started the story of having met him when he was the best friend of my high school boyfriend who has since died, of having tried, after that moment on the bedsteads, to live with him; and it all seemed as I spoke, as so much does these latter days, irrelevant. It was an account, but the account didn't matter, didn't explain. What seemed relevant, although I have no way of explaining this to myself, were the bedsteads and the particular way in which light from a single bulb made the evening simultaneously etched and lost in a kind of washed melancholy which depends,

I am certain, not on the play of memory, although one is tempted to that conclusion, but simply on the light from the lightbulb itself. It was, I thought then and I think now the causal principle for all that followed.

We sat for a long time in that room getting through stories of our failed marriages, and of our children, all of them still at that moment in time, young and fair and about to be dragged, by us, to the Cape for a summer of sun and sand. My son saw a skeleton in the closet there in his room under the dormers which to this day he remembers as if blaming me for something unforgivable.

She said, driving me to his place, not the apartment with the bedsteads and the lightbulb, but to his house some twenty years later, why do you put up with him. She too possesses a character of great certainty, but of an entirely different sort, certain that we should be kind to one another, gentle in our responses, humble and considerate, and since I agree with her, I am uncertain how to convey my sense that it isn't what's called for, that I can't understand (although clearly I do understand in some way) her question nor frame a response. I think of a story that I don't tell.

What does it mean to put up with anyone, with oneself even. How can understanding, whatever that is, be based on the quality of light in a bedroom of an apartment he took after his wife left him to run off to live to this day in Italy and the sun. He tells the story over and over. We sit in his garden, now twenty years later, and he tells the story, not exactly as if it had just happened, but as the single most important event of his life, although both of us know it is not exactly that, although as story it may be. And so, if I say that my husband had an affair with his wife and that when we tried to throw in our lots together that summer on the Cape after sitting all night in a room with the light from a bare lightbulb, it follows that it was doomed to fail. My son came out of the bedroom into the summer sun frightened of the skeleton in the closet and he saw in my child's face the face of the man who had slept with his wife, a fact that might not have mattered so profoundly if his wife had not later left him and run off, but that, given the event and my son's hallucination, mattered enough to change everything that followed.

At least we changed at that moment in which he saw a man in a child's face, changed, as we had to towards one another and I moved away, he bought a large house with a garden and each of us went on to other times and other people who didn't know the stories, or if they did, because we told them, didn't make much of them except as stories. Nor can I really make much more of it all, except to recognize in the story the importance of the elements which imprint themselves on those who live through them rather than hear them recited. Except the slant of light as it came in through the room as my son came out from under the slanted roof to tell the story of the skeleton in his closet. Except as the imprint of light during the telling becomes part of the way stories are

The Lightbulb

passed on from person to person so that while I was in the car with her twenty years later and trying to think of what it meant "to put up with anyone," I was aware of the overcast sky, a sky so unlike the California one I usually live under, that it became part for me of the telling of the story of how his wife had had an affair with my husband and left us, the man and I, forever locked together in a way that isn't "putting up with," but one's life. That the sympathy one feels is, and here of course one is selfish, for oneself, and not only the person one was when young. It isn't, I wanted to explain to her in the car, that you see him as arrogant, or that he is, but rather that I am, I must be or else I forget all the stories of all that has happened and that is far worse than, in an entirely different category from, dominating the conversation.

And since my husband has disappeared, he is also the link to days he has no exact knowledge of, which I may or may not have told him about, but which had to belong to someone other than me and there are, as I said to him in the garden of the house, so few of us left. Few of us, that is, for whom these particular memories matter so much, imprint themselves so fiercely, so that although he wasn't there on the day I learned to make a dramatic mess of things, to throw dishes across the kitchen against the wall, to break the plaster and ruin the dinner and raise my voice so loud the neighbors came down from upstairs in their long johns and laughed and my husband laughed and the old flowered dishes we had found in the closet lay in pieces across the floor, he seems to have participated. And because soon my husband, who needed far more drama than the breaking of dishes or even the making up that followed, would have an affair with his wife and would leave the man standing some years later staring at the face of my son in disbelief that he could look so like the father, if that's what it's called when each of us fails the other out of following a story into a life.

And of course, one keeps trying to get back into that room with the lightbulb, not only because one wishes, as all human beings wish, to turn back the clock, have a chance to do it over again, nor because we think that we might work it all out better, but because we wish to see again. Knowing as one knows that we have all changed through time, we wonder what it was like to be in that room with the exact light from the lightbulb and to listen to oneself say things about the way the marriage failed because I could not learn to speak in ways so foreign to my own, couldn't pick up the drama or extend the range of my voice often or far enough. He told me about how lost he felt, like wandering through mazes underground in the dark he said, without purpose or anchor or children. She had taken the children and we were sitting that evening under the lightbulb on the two beds he had bought for his children if they returned, if she agreed to send them for the summer, if she would get them on the plane from Italy to the United States to this room which seemed once I had heard the story,

The Lightbulb

emptier than before, desolate even, so that the quality of the light changed from being the sort of light I might have imagined for a setting in a café where we might have been sitting over watery beer telling our stories for the camera, to a children's bedroom without the children in a certain unforgettable cast of light.

—∞—

The Ring

She tried to remember but couldn't. Had she sold the ring they'd given her? The whole ordeal seemed murky, missing, irresponsible. Had she been aggressive or so pissed off that they tried to make her what she wasn't? Her toes hit a snag in the sheets; she couldn't sleep in the rolling around of trying to remember the sequence, the shape of things hidden in drawers, from herself, now from them, and what came back were the irrelevant but perhaps meaningful moments earlier when she'd hidden the ring in her apartment since it was so valuable, and then couldn't remember exactly where she'd put it, could see herself, a furtive creature moving here and there, looking in cupboards and boxes and then giving up, taking up something else equally pressing or I'll get to it later, she must have thought.

And then had forgotten for months that she had hidden it since she feared wearing it in public—too showy, too expensive, too at odds with jeans and t-shirts—and then only by chance opening a drawer in the kitchen and finding it wrapped in tissue paper where, she realized, she must have put it, although when exactly, she couldn't recall. Now she squirmed, mortified and sweaty under the summer sheets, rubbing at the ragged skin of her cuticles as if that would clear her head of the ways things hid away and didn't hide, showing up in these nightly vagaries that seemed these days to define her. See what I am, she spoke to them silently and turned over to find not what she was looking for.

In the motel she and the man took out plastic cards and opened the room and fell into the bed and grabbed each other in a rush of not looking at anything, the plastic cards fallen on the floor. Afterwards while he showered, she hit herself across the right side of her face, an action that made itself known to her only the next day when her jaw ached and in trying to remember why her jaw ached or what deep diseases she might be carrying in her jaw and if she should phone up for an appointment at the clinic, she remembered the plastic cards that turned the little light from red to green and opened the door where she was hit across the right side of her face before she took her turn in the shower. She remembered it like a blurred portrait, the girl turning her head, the hand gray and fuzzy, the camera unsteady in someone else's hand.

She could call up the ring perfectly: a pure white stone set deep in a band of gold. Oh my god, who'd you have to be to wear it, and there before her in her thoughts and on her bedside table the portrait of Madame X, a portrait that she could remember perfectly, not only for its perfection, the scooped out décolleté gown, bare white skin, and long long neck, a vision of opulence and grandeur, but also because of what she couldn't look at or look away from, the diamond shoulder strap fallen off her shoulder, a strap pulled taut and horizontal by her outstretched arm, a woman who could wear anything or take anything off. *Distracted*, it says there in the text, and she put her pointed finger on the page, *willfully distracted*, what does it mean willfully distracted when she knew perfectly well to be distracted meant you weren't responsible, that things happened to you, the strap fell, the events occurred and you just happened to be there, it happened to be your shoulder, your bare skin.

At dinner the two men, her best friends really, the ones she depended on, overmuch she sometimes thought, sat across from her as they always, it seemed, sat across from her, the two of them a pair, she "the odd man out," she'd always said over the years as their lives went on together and she went on trying. Trying to fit into their domesticity, their travels, their vision of how it should be, how she should be and what it was like when the silver was put away and she'd gone home. The gleam of their perfect life hung over her like a sword she was tempted to say and she knew she deserved whatever would happen to her since she'd taken their gift and

The Ring

sold it and knew even as they spoke to her at dinner about how lovely the ring was, how it caught the light, that she couldn't produce it. Her insides cramped. She put down her fork.

She saw with embarrassing exactitude the consignment case at the jewelry store, the placement of each item carefully in the carefully lit case, the things someone had loved, had given, now cast off by changing tastes, divorce, death. Someone who wore the tiny wrist watch with the black velvet band had died; whoever inherited it couldn't imagine herself changing to a jeweled evening watch who never changed anything in her life and never meant to ever again.

She must have sold it for some important reason, but she couldn't remember the reason, it was lost in her furtive selling of it in a pinch, but had it been a pinch really or had she had to unloose herself from the demands of splendor, and then she knew she was lying to herself about something, squirreling something away, keeping it shut up in the dark. And yet now it was many years ago, and she hadn't told them and it had gone on for so long it was like forgetting, not so much the event itself, but something, some reason, some aftermath, and the image of the sword returned, too true, too false. She was the one who had taken their generosity and tossed it away and she tried to think of being that person or any person at all. She stood at the sink washing up after a perfect meal. She balanced the silver knife in her hands, the weight of it now wrapped in a tea towel, dried and put away in the left hand drawer.

They'd agreed on the motel because of its funny name, The Farmer's Daughter. It appealed to their sense of the ridiculous made-up quality of their affair, LA architecture veering first in this direction and then that, the names of streets calling up film stars and parades, the motels catching innocence in a name, or was it the gossiped randiness of the daughter, breasts like melons, stuck in the country, up for anything, up for grabs. It was sleazy enough despite the plastic keys and the clean plastic sheeting on the tables, and when they were done and he had left, she calmly hit herself across the right side of the face and felt calmer than she had before and took a long slow shower, drying herself between the toes with the rough towel, having been told that to prevent jet lag one must shower immediately and wipe between all fingers and toes, and every time she did it, she thought of flying, of flying off, of flying into space, of being space itself.

Madame Gautreau, the elegant woman in the painting impressed itself on her, literally *on* her she would have said, and she kept the book open on the stand next to her bed. Even when she thought she'd had enough, she found herself sitting and staring. She looked at the woman. Identified only as Madame X to hide her true identity, she was, nevertheless, someone willing to give over to public display, her ear a purplish pink, the hair

The Ring

swept up, her head turned as if forced over her bare shoulder, gorgeous, haughty, atrocious. It made her skin itch and flake, that white powder as if spilling all over her, but for the purple ear beneath her upswept hair, even then people couldn't stay away, stared at her portrait helplessly.

They said she shouldn't wear the ring with anything but black, a long black dress they imagined she would be a figure of sorts, but she never wore dresses, couldn't grasp the exposure of them. She was wrong, wrong not only in the act itself, walking into the jewelry store and putting her gift in with the other discarded things, sad for the specters of other lives and other times, but also in the forgetting, as if, as she had so often done, she simply couldn't look at what she had done in a past that seemed sketchily put together, remembered only in blurry bits, the walking into the store, the laying out of the pale stone on the counter, the woman wearing a matching two-piece outfit of rose flowers, shoes coordinated in beige and a large ornate crucifix around her neck. It hung there, that dead man on the silver cross. The woman looked into her eyes and smiled, *of course, dear,* and took it and set it in with the other jewels of past lives under the glass topped case like a public viewing before a funeral.

Whenever he got up from the bed and brushed the side of her face with a hand before he went to the shower, she thought of the portrait as helplessly as she lifted her own hand. His arms were white as ice and though she knew they were hers at the moment she knew she couldn't have them, couldn't keep them, wouldn't, perhaps, want them. They had gone now into the shower, and she remembered them only by recalling the portrait at the end of the hall, her white arms hanging at the sides of her black dress, her jewels, her regal neck. She held the piece of plastic in her hand. After a few minutes she remembered it was used to open the door.

But she couldn't remember the year or why she had decided to sell it, why she would get rid of something so beautiful and what she needed the money for, although she often thought she needed money. What had been, she wondered, important enough and she couldn't remember although she thought perhaps it was when she was trying to make a life with someone. Wasn't she always trying to make a life with someone. Who was it she wondered as she turned in the sheets. The pit of her stomach hurt and her mind refused to come up with the face of anyone but the woman in the elegant shop, *yes dear,* she said, as if jewels were dead things without histories or the arthritic hands moving over the sheets, enlarging all her rings, her too many rings, and holding her too tight whenever she came to visit, arriving in the ugly car she always drove. Of course it was wrong, the whole idea of her coming was wrong, how was she to stand it, this woman with the perfume that

The Ring

came at you even days later from a towel left hanging, from an unexpected drawer. Too many rings, too many bracelets, the blue on her eyelids lifting off and floating like a butterfly, and she knew herself queasy, saw it go back to its place on her mother's face.

In the motel she had met him for another late afternoon when he could get free. His face was turned away from her once they were done and she couldn't see it and for one awful moment she couldn't remember which face would turn around when he got up for the shower and before it was her turn and the blur of one face superimposed on another frightened her and gave her an exhilaration far beyond the sex which was, she thought, an excuse for something else anyhow. This time she hit herself before he had left the room and they never came back to that room or any other as it turned out, although neither of them talked to the other or called or tried to sort it out, and she contented herself with returning to the mockery of the motel's name and the scandal of the farmer's daughter, pregnant and abandoned in a small Midwestern town she had to leave, carrying her cardboard suitcase to the train station under her arm like Kim Novak. The sting left a reddish mark on the right side.

She felt tired and faint and lost in the details of what she could remember and the wash of what she couldn't, and somehow nothing could pull her out of this feeling or keep her now from sleep and almost sleep and the irritation of coffee she tried to drink and couldn't and the overwhelming colors that engulfed her. Could she have acted so, like a slap in the face to the men she depended on, to whom she must have wanted to return, the table set, the candles lit, the silver gleaming. She thought if she stayed here looking at the portrait, there'd be no more memories, only the perfection of Mme Gautreau holding herself erect and aloof no matter who stared at her, came to gawk.

The red of the floppy roses on the woman's suit hurt her eyes and she smelled the color of white as if talc had invaded the room, her nose, her eyes itched with the perfume chalk of it. The sound of the soprano's voice was high-pitched and grating. Red and green clicked on and off. Here she was as she thought she'd always been, bloated and tired and outlandish, the object of ridicule and shame. She kept thinking of the little plastic card that lit up the green light in the motel room. A little jewel of light. It was something she didn't want to see now and she didn't want to see ever again.

Part 2

La Belle Dame

He sat at the edge of things trimming words out of paragraphs in his mind. His wife on the other hand laid a table for six with purple candles and lit them and straightened them and stood back to look at them and straightened them again. He paid no attention to the candles or anything else. She glared at him without animosity. He trimmed off "releasing the double meaning on principle." I watched. I wanted to put my hands on the top of his bald head the way I always do. Why is it that men fear going bald, when it is exactly this trait which makes them erotic, so available and irresistibly blank. One can't touch men in any way really—they have such good defenses—but when they are bald, it is as if one had a head on a platter without the fuss of dancing or veils.

When the other guests arrived we sat down for conversation and wine and we all started in, I with some usual enthusiasm, this time a fixation on a poem

I'd just read, the others about a conference on semiot-
ics. Somewhere in the city, papers were still being read,
speeches given. He tried to join in, but his paragraph,
the one he had been working on, held him tight in her
arms; you could almost see him struggle to get loose,
but it was of no avail. One loopy sentence drifted like
tendrils around him. The rhapsody of thought held him
in thrall, La Belle Dame etc., and no matter that he made
himself look straight at us, he couldn't see us, and we
remained that lumpy and indistinguishable blur called
"dinner guests."

> O *what can ail thee, knight at arms*
>   *Alone and palely loitering?*
> *The sedge has wither'd from the Lake*
>   *And no birds sing.*

One can't help being sympathetic with one so lost
in his own thoughts, removed, so unable to join in. I
tried to throw looks of sympathy his way as I thumbed
through photographs of the family and family dog being
passed around. One can't help one's fondness for the
specific: the sleek head of the Doberman, the missing
teeth of the small boy. But for the most part, and this
remained throughout the evening, I couldn't get over
the prominence of his head and the glorious abstraction of his mind. I couldn't stop thinking about what it
meant to live inside one's head, to have vast capacities of
thought, to be able to follow one's roving ideas through

potential paragraphs and pages, despite dinner guests. I think that if it had been in his control, he would have joined in and would in fact have enjoyed the company his wife had gathered together to eat pasta on shiny blue plates. She too was Italian and a great cook, everybody said so, and the guests were witty enough, charming and eager, leaning forward over their blue plates, semiotic quips, ties and beads. But as it was, he was lost on the edges of who could ever imagine what brilliant ideas, what perfectly orchestrated arguments.

One has to, one friend says to me, one just has to, if only from time to time, use one's best china. The watery blue that linked us over the years of our friendship expanded and flowed around us as the evening progressed: the purple candles, the blue plates, the mood of sentimental intelligence, the fact of our having had so many dinners together over so many years. What we knew or thought we knew about each other. So the wash of the evening was as the watery wash of the brush over colors too saturated, too refined. We all blended and purred.

After a while he couldn't even pretend. His mouth stopped its silent opening and shutting as if he might possibly join in, his eyes stopped trying to focus, his hands began a silent dance of gestures meant, I am sure, to illustrate the points he was making in the paragraph he was writing or had written or thought to write when a break finally came and he could escape from the swaying of the crowd.

Once as a child I took a dance class, not the usual ballet I was used to, but a special session offered on Saturday by a special guest teacher from Albany. We stood in our black leotards, all ungainly girls, all unformed and shy, and were asked to become a forest of trees, to sway to the music with our arms outspread, to bend and blend together as if our branches were being swept by incessant wind. There was no way, despite our embarrassment, not to do what we were told to do (we were obedient and trained, after all, good girls with identical topknots and feeble aspirations), swaying and bending in a way that we knew already by the age of nine was out of date and stupid. Does it mean not being stupid, this life of the mind, this fervor to stand alone, to pursue a thought to its finish, to finish a line of argument or recall a poem while everyone else is finishing dessert or clearing the table or swaying to the music. He was like a rock in the middle of the stream. We all moved around him as if he were insensate matter, as if his head were the boulder, as if he were only a sign pointing elsewhere, not to us, not to any of us. His wife poked teasingly, familiarly at his ribs at about the middle of the dinner, but finally gave up, acquiesced, and his silence became the most obvious part of the conversation, not that we stopped or faltered, intent as we were on discussing the roast beef, the rosemary potatoes, and the lemon pie—its glaze reflecting back the watery light of the candles—but that it was incorporated as part of the whole piece we were constructing, until by the end of the evening I was exhausted beyond all manner of thinking by the sheer effort of stepping around him, not including him, not hearing his voice, not expecting a response.

I felt myself sweaty and wet with the effort of ignoring the head that was so prominent and fine. I too, I too, I wanted to say. I know what you're like. I too am alone. I too embrace abstract thought; I too can quote Keats. I knew what he was thinking, could feel the difficulty of transition, of how to capture the range of meanings, the sinister proliferation of possible comments about one word. What was the word. I concentrated, but it slipped away: *mutatis mutandis*. And I wanted this head, more than anything else, I wanted to hold it and cradle it and make it my own. To me it had become a valued object, a thing to be possessed and clung to, the only thing worth having—not the thoughts themselves exactly, but their locus, the bald head towering above us as we went about exchanging dates and plans and ideas for the next party, the next grouping of dinner plates.

I'll do green, I promised, *all green*. One New Year's we'd had an all black affair; we'd announced as if in chorus our sophisticated disdain for celebrations of the New Year, our love of the old, our hatred of joy and hats and whistles. Instead, we proposed, we'd go into mourning for the lovely past, wear black for the old year and eat only black food: blackened fish, black pasta with squid ink sauce, blackberries, wine so dark as to seem black. Black olives. I could do all green easily enough, but my heart wasn't in it. I didn't want to plan ahead, didn't want to discuss what salads I'd concoct, where to buy the best arugula. I wanted to watch the bald man quote and trim, add and subtract, think his weighty thoughts and recite poetry. Now he was mouthing an entirely new paragraph, a new projection, had pulled in philosophical ideas to undergird his point, and then had begun, I could see it, to quote the lines themselves:

And there she lulled me asleep,
  And there I dream'd, Ah! woe betide!
The latest dream I ever dreamt
  On the cold hill's side.

I wanted this removed being, this standoffish husband, this owl of a man. What was he doing so all alone on the shores of his thoughts, pacing up and down in the narrow room, furrowing his extensive brow. I wanted to watch him as he slept, watch the head in noble repose. We were, I wanted to tell him, exactly alike. I could read him, I knew it. We were meant for each other. He was alone; I was alone. I meandered up and down *the cold hill's side.*

In such a state, I lost, as one might have expected, my usual ability to concentrate on several things at once, keeping the one tune going while overlaying grace notes, keeping the color clear while adding water, whole brushfuls of clear water. I was no longer able to talk about next Thursday and get the word I was looking for, looking *at*, one might say, as my eyes just grazed the top of his head again and again, knowing the word would appear if I just brushed past it enough times, like rubbing a lead pencil over a paper laid on a tombstone and watching the knight's shield with its hidden meanings come clear. I must have been clearing the table, trying in the ordinary course of things to maneuver just a bit closer to the thoughts I could almost hear *("our literature is thus characterized by the pitiless divorce between the producer of the text and its user, between its owner and its customer, between its author and its reader")*, almost. Dear reader, I broke the platter, it slipped out of my hands on the way to the kitchen and was smashed into a million bits. I almost had hold of the word but the platter got away. *Olive oil*, Sharia said. *It's edges are covered in olive oil. Not to worry*, she said and scrambled and mopped and collected the pieces.

Then, as if the smashed platter had done it, broken the spell and all connection between us, the man laughed and turned to his wife in congratulations for a fine affair, for all her splendid efforts in the kitchen (he congratulated her on the perfection of the roast), and put his arms around her and laughed as if the union of one with another were as easy as anything. The *pale loitering* I had seen so clearly that it seemed etched on the walls of the dining room, vanished. The dog came into the room and hung, sloppy and wet, about the backs of our legs. The boy woke and stood in yellow pajamas at the top of the stairs. The spell was broken, as if one had waked cold and alone on a hill and I, embarrassed and foolish, wrapped myself in my thick winter coat, December in New York, and went home alone by taxi in the dark.

Marybeth and the Fish

Marybeth said vaguely, *They are nice, silvery sort of,* and preened by turning her head and thinking she had hair enough. She saw the words *Veronica Lake* as if written in loopy scroll on her inner eyelids, thought of *Sullivan's Travels*, and came back feeling better from her brief reverie of someone else's blond beauty. Puffy off-the-shoulder blouses were in again. Hers was worn a shade defensively, but in the smoky noise of the gallery opening no one would notice.

Someone compared the work on the wall to Lissitzky but someone said no it was not so ironic, and there was an exchange about what did irony mean anyhow in these post-everything days. Marybeth had always had a suspicion that often it was meanness. From his leather chair, out of the past, her father said something she couldn't quite hear as if the sound on the TV had been turned off. She remembered opening colored pencils in a flip-top box and she remembered laughing with her father at whatever he had said in that long-ago afternoon when afternoons seemed to grow longer and quieter as she made drawing after drawing.

Tom thought she should talk more. He said he liked her way of *getting into the visual component of cooking*, the way she stared at the color of tomatoes as she stirred the spoon around and around. But sometimes he was just irked. Her book covers were elegant and people ordered them and with the job at the café it was enough. She knew what celadon green would do and she mostly took life, except for the occasional pain in her stomach, in a dazed sort of way.

Although she wasn't as sure of herself as most took her to be, she delivered well in a voice high and darty, and used the pain, the small but sharp one, to make a kind of arching stance. It was what, so he said, had drawn Tom to her in the first place. He'd seen her in what he'd called *a delicious mope* one night, but it was the sort of mope edged off by wit. At least it seemed that way to Tom who was hooked he said. Tom's way of putting things seemed to Marybeth as if the shade of color were slightly off. She looked away from the strident fluorescent bouncing off the gallery walls.

I could be wrong, someone said and went for wine. *If anything goes, what sort of standards . . . it's all a realm of play. It's true in fashion, music, I mean I know all that about the failure of institutions but isn't this, I mean, we're not in the nineteenth century.*

Marybeth and the Fish

One whose hair radiated around a bored but pale face opened her mouth. Her girlfriend stuck a cigarette in and began to croon *Stormy Weather. Are you singing these days?* The person speaking felt embarrassed and obliged to ask and she was, at the Club A.V. She'd made it, at least as back-up, so she was stuck where she was. *I just stick to oldies*, she said to no one in particular and passed a hand over the radiant fluff of hair. Both of the women wore black like most in the room but had moved beyond producer-leather. They hummed.

I adore it, the gallery owner said, coming from the back room, expansive and high.

Marybeth was glad she'd gone blank for a moment and glad Tom's work sold but not in this sort of blow-out way. She looked at the gallery owner's French wife and wondered if that was why she didn't seem to mind—pretty enough but no knockout and still she carried it off no matter what he did. Tom was good at what he did and people were always after him, his jeans tight on his thin frame. She wished it reminded her of how fake the world was, but it didn't. Her stomach ached. Rubbing her cheek on the faded cloth as she extended her legs on the couch when they watched TV, she saw the warm color of bits of cloth she'd kept in a box in the closet when she was nine.

Once in a therapy group she said to a man who had a wife, three children, and affairs in his head: *Thinking is the same as doing it*. They said she had to learn to express her anger. She hated his descriptions of free-floating limbs in net stockings over the head of his wife underneath him on the bed, so she recited lessons about the gravity of mortal sin from Catholic school and then felt guilty for having lied, for not saying the man's loose flesh made her ill and that she'd never been a Catholic.

A dark-haired woman was talking to Tom who was twisting his cuff the way he did. Marybeth had thought the affair was over. A man in a narrow suit interrupted her with a drink. His bluish skin was shiny and he was good at talking and slicking back his slicked back hair. Next to him Marybeth felt mute, but her eyes lit up anyhow on cue as he began on the soul-force of *Das Lied von der Erde*. She tried not to watch Tom and Carol as their sentences twinned one another, broke off, and reattached. She tried hard to attend, although she felt herself drowning in the man's enthusiasm and he was in any case speaking to some audience somewhere she was a mere stand-in for. She tried to remember the last classical music she had heard. He said something she missed. She shut her eyes and saw a watercolor of a dark-haired woman turning into a hare. Across the room she recognized a painter she knew who was staggering and who wouldn't come with them later but would go back to his room, liquor his particular form of discipline.

Her own life was tidy enough. She hunted plastic from the 50's, Bakelite spoons, green glass plates. She could see teacups and saucers on the sill above the sink.

Marybeth and the Fish

The last book she'd done had been turned, flyleaf out, the speckle across the outside, admired, a talk at a local college, a mild sort of fame. She wished she were sitting down when she saw Tom's wrists fold.

Too brightly she came up to where Tom was standing. *Carol's coming with us,* he said, putting an arm around her shoulder in a gesture that might have been reassuring. *We might do an installation together. Want any more?* Marybeth shook her head. Carol said yes and Tom left them standing together.

Oh, it's nothing, Carol said to someone passing by, turning her head to sweep the room and fixing the corner where Tom stood with empty glasses and a man in a ponytail whose arms filled what space there was. Carol smiled as the owner slid by to set her glass earring swinging and to say something about her last video. *I want to show you something,* he said and slid some more, pulling her with him towards the back room pulling his tweed jacket off in the heat, leaving Marybeth standing alone.

Marybeth knew she was pretty enough but at the moment it didn't help. The cupboards she had painted appeared somewhere. A woman in white bumped her out of it and she wondered if it was being older. She kept losing her sense of how funny it was in spite of losing weight.

At the restaurant she ordered a dish from the vegetable column that wouldn't stay with her too long. She wouldn't have chosen to come here but this year

Korean was in again. Others ordered portions of raw meat with garlic, transparent noodles, a stir-fried squid, potstickers, a whole barbecued fish. Everyone wanted something. A women told a story about a screenwriter who had churned out a screenplay for a joke and made pots of money. *Did you like the work,* someone tried again. They looked around to see if the artist had arrived. A friend of Tom's Marybeth couldn't remember drank in the corner. He looked out of an old movie, perhaps on purpose. She thought about the purposeful and love and then tried not to.

The waiters set dishes down in front of each person who flipped aside purses, hair, scarves, jackets, in order to get at the food and reordered beer and pushed chairs to sit by the right person in the confusion of who had ordered what. Carol began a story about her last show and everyone's eyes turned on her. She could get anyone to do anything and anyone to listen. You just had to watch her mouth form words. Marybeth tried to see the color of the end piece she wanted to use on the book she was designing. She brushed her hand as if by accident on Tom's jeans as he moved to help with bottles of beer and remembered something. She tried to pull it into herself and gather herself as if it were not elsewhere but here. The food was pungent and loud, chopped and steaming. Marybeth looked down at what was set in front of her and into the gaping mouth of a toothy fish.

I think that's mine, Carol laughed, reaching. Marybeth felt her voice tuning itself high and darty.

Marybeth and the Fish

She remembered something else and her father. *No,* she said, putting a large piece of garlic and fish in her mouth and biting down hard. She knew her stomach would hurt but not until tomorrow.

Blue/Green

*Nature is on the inside, says Cézanne. Quality, light, color, depth,
which are there before us, are there only because they awaken an
echo in our body and because the body welcomes them.*

—Merleau-Ponty

For a long time her favorite color was blue. It simply
was her favorite color, and she couldn't stand orange—
the color of cheap lipstick and being kissed when you
didn't want to be, hard and wet. A book of lies in a grease
stick. But blue was the color of skies you could lie under
and watch the clouds overhead and the color of violets
underfoot when you walked in the woods or by the side
of the river or in bouquets handed out by the poor little
match girl to some gentleman who passed by in tails
wearing his heart on his sleeve on late night TV.

So she concocted a theory about why people collect
things of a certain color, why they gather them up in
piles, why the woman with obvious skill at needlepoint

also has a house filled with blue glass objects, so many there is no way to grasp whether or not they are beautiful individually or even as a group, since there are so many of them that it's the magnitude you note, not even the blue particularly except they are, of course, all blue. You collect things, then, she supposed, because they evoke a whole side of yourself that opens and opens inside and out, or perhaps because the sheen or the shape sets off something you can't get enough of, like that warm shoulder you are leaning against. Or it's a Cézanne. I love you, you say.

Psychological theories about sexual magnetism are all wet, she was sure of it, they don't take the color of things into account. This one razors his hair and overdyes it blond; his much older friend who longs for him does the same. It's color theory that's essential and will finally allow us to make sense of why someone sticks around. Some aesthetic faculty kicks in and one is transfixed, so the philosopher says. Things *have an internal equivalent in me; they arouse in me a carnal formula of their presence. Color is the place where our brain and the universe meet.*

So there she was, marching about and theorizing randomly, in that oblivious way of youth, and liking blue and buying blue shirts, blue jeans, blue silk scarves. She was walking in the blue twilight, singing a version of *Blue Moon*. It defined and contained her and she thought that this sort of thing would go on forever, or if not forever, at least until she was much older. Then she'd see. But then, one day she realized that blue was the color of adolescence, it was watching television all afternoon and waiting for the phone to ring or poking at your skin in a pretense of martyrdom.

And it was green in fact that took her, penetrated, amazed. She looked in a mirror, not, of course, being acutely self-conscious, that she hadn't spent hours looking at herself, her eyebrows, the slope of her brow, but that she saw, suddenly, something different: herself in some form she hadn't seen before. Her own optic system shifted and she couldn't see blue anymore and preferred green instead, a sort of muddy gray-green, the color of celadon pottery, the color of certain mosses in a tangle of dark branches, a color that drew you to it and made you want to stand next to it the way certain people make you want to match shoulders with them just to feel the warm side of a certain arm.

The certain arm turned out to belong to Marnie. She wanted to go where Marnie was and she wanted to *be* Marnie. There was no particular reason why this was the woman she wanted to be. It just was. One might explain it and one might explain it in several ways. She was blond. She had that name. And she seemed to possess a blithe insouciance, whatever that was, and to walk about like a boy, guileless and effortlessly physical as often boys can be. That's it, she thought. She wanted to lope. She wanted greenish shirts and a dog. She wanted to write about the vastness of the mountain air.

Blue/Green

One day in the middle of summer she went to where Marnie was vacationing in the country and simply wouldn't go away. She'd invited herself against all protests and had gotten in the car and arrived. Marnie found it odd, this person who appeared out of nowhere wouldn't leave and kept staring at her as if she were being, not desired exactly, but examined so that the imitation would be as correct as possible. Marnie thought: perhaps she's attracted to me, perhaps that's it. But she seemed just to want to copy like a schoolgirl, like girls she once knew who dressed alike and had to have the same book covers or running shoes.

On that afternoon, despite the oddity of it, they went for a walk with the dog, fed the chickens, and returned to the cabin to eat the various cheeses she had brought for the occasion, a small bribe for coming uninvited Marnie supposed, and they sat around and got a little drunk, not too drunk, but drunk enough in the perfect way of certain women, and ate small amounts of goat cheese on very thin crackers. They talked about things that mattered to them both in a sort of hum, as if talk were not exchange, but a matching of tones and tonal shifts. They talked of quality, color, light, and what each had thought about the ways the light fell on the rooftops, the platters of fruit, the painting, *La Route Tournante en Sous-Bois*. They puckered their mouths over the slightly sour cheese.

Of course, as you have no doubt realized by now, if someone wants to be another, the other often also wants to be her. At the museum you stand in front of the painting of *Les Baigneurs* and you shift into the pose in front of you, tilt this way or that. There is no rational explanation, and no reason why one likes green now but blue before, no reason why it is wonderful one day to drive so fast on the freeway you can only think of speeding faster and faster onto new and more precipitous bridges, crossing over the expanses of asphalt as fast as the car will go, and then you don't want that at all. Why would anyone go faster than the speed limit? Why would anyone break any rule of the road? Why would anyone wear anything other than a uniform, if not one prescribed by the nuns or military officers, then one of one's own choosing: *only* Nehru collars, perfectly out of date since they are still worn without irony by serious young men too thin for their own good, *only* bowling shirts, *only* jackets one size too large, *only* one-piece bathing suits. Why would one put one's hand on that particular object and sense a settling as if the winds had finally given up.

Once when she was a girl she wanted to be a girl named Grace because her name was Grace, and she knew it would alter her entire way of looking at the world. In the photograph she keeps with the others on her bureau, Grace stands at the side of a lake at a camp they went to one summer, her head tilted to the side, her ponytail hanging into the sunlight that fractures her ponytail, her face, and an incandescent smile.

You wish you could unlock the muscles across the top of your shoulders and you think, if only I were

134

someone else, they wouldn't have locked in the first place. She couldn't help it most of the time, she simply found herself, often embarrassingly, copying the gestures of another, imitating the tone of someone's voice, responding to the clerk with an accent in a similar accent, using a certain word or phrase which clearly belonged to someone else. In response to a question, her mouth formed an echo, an echo that seemed oddly beautiful as if to lose a "t" made the word smooth as rocks worn by water. She hoped no one would notice, and certainly Marnie wouldn't since it was her idea, she thought, it was she who had introduced this idea into the conversation, at least she thought it was. During the entire afternoon, they drew on one another constantly, walking slowly down the path, side by side, shoulder by shoulder. She quoted a poem as if to explain, *The mind, that ocean where each kind/ Does straight its own resemblance find;/ Yet it creates, transcending these,/ Far other worlds and other seas,/ Annihilating all that's made/To a green thought in a green shade.*

Both changed clothes, then exchanged clothes, though it hardly mattered by then since they were both wearing castoffs from the trunk in the cabin someone else had left behind. It rained, their other clothes were wet, so they reasoned, and the clothes belonged to both and to no one. This is the thing about explanations, there are always some lying about.

When Marnie woke in the morning she wondered if her small gifts had been diminished or if she were just a bit hung-over from wine in the afternoon. She, for her part, thought her hair a bit paler, though she knew this was a ridiculous notion. No one's hair turns overnight.

What does one afternoon count for after all. Yet the one afternoon left them all they could think of. She looked out at the sky and saw that in the gathering storm it had turned a color tilting towards green. It stood out from all other afternoons in its awkwardness and tears. At one point, each looked at the other, squirmed and blinked, and looked away. They stood shoulder to shoulder, one a bit higher than the other. They measured the height of the wall and then themselves as if it mattered and it made them think of something funny, though neither laughed, simply shifted their legs beneath them at the oddity, at scrutiny, at loss and gain. She knew all this, of course. Yet she knew that her manner of speaking had changed and that there was nothing she could do about it. She knew without a doubt that she had never used the word *happiness* before in her life. She'd always felt it beneath her, something for others rather more superficial and glib than she. Yet what was that odd olive green—she turned towards the window to take it in again—but happenstance expanded across the entire sky. She had been so infused with the new color, she thought, that one thing might lead to another.

—∞∞∞—

Their Calendar

It was when my parents decided they could live with the blue plastic furniture left behind in the house they bought, I knew something was wrong. You don't just go from antiques to unquestioned acceptance of the inevitable like that. I said so too. Over the years they'd picked things up here and there that belonged to them and to my childhood. On a drive into Vermont they'd snagged a leather bellows for the fireplace and bought a contraption no one could figure out what it was and lined it with copper and used it for liquor bottles so people standing around could wonder what it was or when were they ever in that neck of the woods.

After retirement, they decided to move to Florida for some reason I could never fathom. What are you thinking, I said, aghast at the whole idea. Why are you going, I'd say, and why Florida of all places. I tried to say it was hard to make friends at their age and how they should stay close by just in case and how finding doctors in new places wasn't easy, but they didn't seem to hear. It was like talking to the wall. They began making arrangements, not impetuously—they never did anything like that—but arrangements nevertheless, as if in slow motion. I'd stop by after work but they never seemed to need anything. A box tied and sealed stood by the front door. After a while there was another. The house grew emptier and my voice echoed. I thought things had been sent ahead but when I arrived later to help there was almost nothing to unpack and the house still clung to stray remnants from the former occupants.

Everything was ugly: the light blue wake of a shag rug, the plastic chairs, the cartoon pelican that smirked from its frame in the bathroom, the dusty wreath made of pale pink shells. And these few awful things were overwhelming because, as I said, when we came to unpack it turned out they'd brought almost nothing of their own. They said for me not to come but I was duty bound it seemed to me and how could I let them to do it alone and so I flew down the first chance I could get. But there was almost nothing to do. I remembered a house I grew up in, heavy, dark furniture filling every room, and at Christmas endless balls and lights for the Christmas tree, but this time they decided to "travel light" they said and had sold off what they'd collected and left behind not only holidays but almost everything I remembered. Even the dresser that had been a dentist's cabinet was still in Connecticut and I had to give up what I thought would be my lifelong curiosity about how many times a sock had to be folded before it would fit in the narrow drawer.

They brought one photo of each relative and gave away all the rest. I had the awful thought of myself lying around in a dusty junk store box for years, and then found by a stranger who wanted to see what we looked like back then in those funny clothes. And they picked out the worst of the lot. His sister wore the dotted dress no one had ever liked. The one of me is especially bad. I am twelve, need braces, and have a raw nose from a bad cold. I haven't yet grown into my size. At forty, I'm still a big girl but all the flesh comes to sit better as the years pass and I know how to dress and well, I still look good for my age. The salesgirls all say I can wear the sorts of dresses I've always worn.

I thought they'd get more stuff fairly soon, things to match the casual retirement I imagined for them, but they didn't. All they did was rip out the lawn, circle the house in gravel and get two stray lawn chairs to face the ocean. They sat there as if waiting for something.

They were oddly uncommunicative, not that they ever were very good at talking, but now they had given up even the small talk of the breakfast table. It was as if they were communicating by the mere passing of salt and pepper, by some sort of sign that passed between them. The doling out of the newspaper went on as usual but it was as if they had mastered something or refined it so that I found myself chattering on about, well, at that time, it was the local elections to my school board, but it was as if I were speaking to the air. He would nod or say yes, but it was as if the idea of whole sentences had dropped out of their universe. I'd always had to do most of the work, bringing anecdotes from the office to cheer them up, telling jokes I'd got off e-mail. I like stories now and again and finding out about the news. Maybe I am a bit used to talking down, working at the middle school and all, but I've got an eye and usually can bring anyone out. But this was downright peculiar.

When she alters my skirts, Marie says she likes my way of telling things the best of all her customers. I notice things, where the best sales are, who recently painted his house, the name on the mailbox next door, who's put in the best new rose. But I can't even get them to visit in the neighborhood, despite the news I bring back from my walks, and it's not too bad, really, little houses in a row and the water there to look at. It's a good site, I tell them, a good investment, values can only go up and you meet such nice people. I talked to the neighbor on the beach who has found two quarters already with his metal detector. I would have preferred the bayside myself, the water is warmer and there is nothing like a warm swim, I say, buoyed up and surrounded by salt water and the blue of the sky. I told them I would also have liked it better nearer the shops and I keep trying to get her out of the house to go shopping. It will do you good, I say, and besides it looks as if you left most of your clothes behind. Where is the red sweater I got you for the retirement party, I ask, a bit of a gathering

Their Calendar

I organized in spite of their protests. Well, it just isn't right to ignore such important occasions. Though they said they didn't want a fuss, I just knew they'd want to see old friends, have the usual toasts and best wishes and cut the cake: *Happy Golden Years* it said in red and gold frosting.

I pushed the hangers aside thinking something must be on the shelves behind, but they were as empty as the kitchen drawers. I hunted for things I had handled forever, it seems, through my childhood, but they had gone to charity, she said over her shoulder. That's how she talked to me as if she could only project at an angle while moving into the next room as if she had something to do, but when she got there she wasn't doing anything. I'd come in after her and find her standing as if she were listening to something. Got a seashell in your ear, I'd say, but she didn't seem to hear or find it funny.

And she bought odd food, none of my favorites. I found a fish store in town and talked to the manager about how we liked halibut and he said we were on his ready list. But she went to the supermarket and bought a freezer full of Lean Cuisine and said she couldn't be bothered. When you opened a drawer there was one thing in it, a fork or a bottle cap or a plastic bag, folded as if it had been washed and ironed.

She bought a bottle of soy sauce and stuck it at the top of a cupboard I couldn't reach and no one likes Chinese food anyhow. I've never been fond of foreign cooking, could never take to it really. It seems such a lot of trouble and you're always hungry right after anyhow or have a headache and besides I like hearty things—*you are a hearty girl*, she used to say to me—and Thanksgiving dinners especially. I loved coming home for dinner and even when mom asked if I didn't sometimes want to visit friends or take a bit of my vacation in my free time from teaching, I preferred really to come home for mashed potatoes and where the heart is.

He was reading. It was a magazine I'd seen him with before, and it didn't look as if he were really reading, but using it as a kind of prop. You know: *someone who is reading needs a magazine.* I tried to start up with him, but I just couldn't get a response. Some people, and he is like that, just won't answer when they're sitting in a certain chair with a certain look no matter how one tries. I'm one for getting a giggle out of people and I've collected my share of witty remarks over the years, but nothing worked. I've always been one to try. Try, try again is my motto. That's why I was so good a swimmer as a girl and was on the swim team in high school, the photo of it on my bedroom wall, a blue frame, you know, for water.

I started out trying to explain new recipes to mom, especially the new ones I'd just put in her file folder, but she just wouldn't go over them. She was getting ready to do it she said, but then I just found her standing as if she couldn't remember what to do next and not getting ready for anything. Everything stayed the same after those first few days. The stuff the Baxters had left just stayed; the boxes would have stayed in the hall if I hadn't flattened them and bundled them for the collection.

The calendar stayed turned to July though it was August, and when I moved to change it, he just stared hard at me as if he knew something I didn't. My hand lifted towards the page, but I couldn't do it, as if I'd forgotten what I was about to do, well not exactly forgotten, but I didn't tear the month from the wall. At home I rule off each day with a sharp pencil. I was willing, of course, to do anything they asked, but it was as if they had arrived at a place with rules already set and didn't want to upset the given order of things, were studiously following a prescribed routine. The chairs were too far apart for conversation, but they didn't want them moved. They could have been upside down for all they seemed to care.

Maybe, I thought, they've just been alone too long, maybe they're just getting old. They weren't depressed exactly though I do like a perky person to be around and I tried to bring some life into the house. I tried to get mom to join me in decorating the wastebaskets with pictures I cut from *National Geographic*. She didn't say no, she just didn't sit down at the card table with me. Something momentous seemed about to be revealed. Nonsense, I said to myself, thinking these sorts of thoughts is what makes people act the way *they* were acting. I decided on a brisk walk to the pier where I talked to people who naturally brightened at my company. I learned all of their names before they had to rush off to collect shells, they said, or would gladly have stayed. I have that way about me, I can bring out most anybody. You can find a common topic with anyone if you try and here there's always the weather or the birds. Everyone wants to see the roseate spoonbill at the bird sanctuary, and you can always talk about that. I myself like to watch them feeding in the mud at low tide even though it means getting up ever so early.

When I came back they were sitting in the gravel in the two chairs looking at the sunset. It was a pretty one, but I just couldn't bring myself to interrupt whatever it was they were doing, though of course as far as I could tell they weren't and wouldn't ever be doing anything. I went inside for a cool drink which I always have after a walk—to rehydrate after even mild exercise is important for one's health I always say—and I saw the calendar again. When I went to tear off the month, though, I saw his face again as it was before, frozen and silent in front of me, and I felt suddenly too big for some reason and in the way, though there was nothing to be in the way of so far as I could tell. I don't know, I just never got around to fixing the calendar then or later. It stayed with the red number marking the Fourth as if it were always going to be July.

The Flea Market

She tried to point out to him the tricky consequences of kindness, but he just didn't get it. She, however, wanted to get this idea across, although if you'd asked her why, she couldn't have explained. It had mostly to do with his ex-wife to whom he was, at least as far as she could tell, devoted, patient and very kind. She, the one doing the explaining, thought he should be respectful and polite, but did he have to go out of his way. After all, the divorce was final, they had no children, no pets, and no debts. It should have been over, she thought.

It turned out they did have, however, a vast array of furniture, more couches and chairs and lamps and rugs and bureaus and plein-air paintings than she had ever seen. The ex-wife was a flea-market junkie. Every Sunday she set out with a wire basket on wheels to the Rose Bowl flea market and came home laden with art treasures. She was passionate about it and had thought early on in the marriage that eventually and with coaxing, he would become passionate too, that they would do this together and, she had imagined, would gaze in rapture at the tree which in the odd painting she'd picked up last week looked positively anthropomorphic, a cypress, curiously bent and dull green. It was more than beautiful, this throbbing thing. Something tore at her heart, lit up her skin, propelled her into the next week when she could do it again. And she had done this every Sunday of every month of every year they had been married until their house, now his house, was filled to the brim and overflowing into the garage, the storage shed, the basement.

She had left him because he had no taste and also, she proclaimed, no passion. *What are you up to, what do you want, I mean, really want*, she asked with fervor. *You can't just wander in the world hiking and liking only trees. It's too vague; it isn't enough.* The one explaining the cruelty of being kind said that just liking trees was fine with her, and so he and she got on well in a mild but satisfying sort of way for the most part, except for his kindness and refusal to confront the issue of bag and baggage.

The ex-wife had moved out into a small apartment in Santa Monica. *It's for the air*, she said and breathed with satisfaction the way people who live on the other side of the 405 freeway do. Soon she had filled up the small apartment with paintings of trees, the painted kind being, as she explained, far more real and valuable. She had, everyone had to admit, a quite splendid collection and she hung the walls with them and stuffed them under the couch and put them cheek by jowl and just everywhere until it was impossible to move except in the narrow passage between front door and kitchen. She invited him over for viewings and she kept on. Later, she called from the road. She had five large framed ones and the oak table had to be bought, had to be carted home, had to be lifted into the back of her SUV and he had to help and he, being kind, did.

Not only did she not give up her passion for collecting, she also refused to give up her passion to convey to him her passion for collecting and for the beauty of the painted trees, the artificial color of the foliage, the arrangements of shapes and vacancies, the ways in which they were, she explained carefully, superior to trees in general. Tears formed in her eyes. She called him to meet her for lunch. Over tomato sandwiches she went over the composition of the newest painting in great detail. She so wanted him to understand. Just try to see it, she said. Just try. Her eyes were bright. Like the gleam of paint in the corner, he thought, and wondered why he had had such a thought. He wondered why he had never seen it before and why it made him feel, as he rarely felt, unsettled.

The one doing the explaining about cruelty and kindness wanted to move in with the man with the ex-wife, but she wanted, she explained patiently, to move into a house they could make their own, not one laden with the paraphernalia of another, the mirrors of another, the draperies and rugs and tastes of another. *She needs to get on with her life by herself, you know,* she said. *Couldn't you,* she asked, *get her to clear out?* But the man couldn't explain why not. *You don't want to hurt her, is that it? I don't, of course,* he said, *want to hurt her,* although that wasn't exactly it, he knew; he just didn't know how to explain. *It's her passion and her life. It's what keeps her going, I don't know what she'd do without it, and well, I couldn't take it away, now could I,* he asked. He didn't, he realized without knowing why, mention what he'd seen in the corner of the painting, the gleam that kept floating disconcertingly before his eyes.

You wouldn't want me to, would you? I would, she wanted to say, but it was the wrong thing to say or at least the wrong time. So, instead, she tried to explain, as if explaining would straighten things out, that if he kept on being kind, his ex-wife would never strike out on her own, would always call on him at inopportune moments, would continue to dominate his life, *our* life, she slipped in, although it was a word neither had used before. Her usually mild voice moved in the direction of complaint. She said, *You need to do something,* and he said he would but he didn't and she tried again to explain that his being kind was a kind of cruelty, and he said, *You don't understand,* which she didn't.

One Sunday she suggested they take a hike and look at trees in the nearby mountains and he would have liked to, he said, yes, he would have, and he said this in such a way as not to hurt her feelings, except he

The Flea Market

had promised to be on call in case his ex-wife couldn't get the garden set she'd hoped to find at the flea market home without help. *She's been after it for quite some time,* he told her. *It's what she says she really wants more than anything and the dealer promises it will be there today. There is no garden at her apartment,* the explainer explained, and then she found herself caught in the folds of what she was saying. *There is,* she went on helplessly, *only a garden at your house.* And she finally understood, without its being explained, something more about the extraordinarily tricky nature of kindness.

Hands

Let me not to the marriage of true minds
Admit impediments.

—William Shakespeare, Sonnet 116

Too grim is what we all thought about Sam, Samantha, too caught up in endeavors to be artistic, thrusting poems at friends and strangers alike, ignoring the everyday stuff of what can be gathered up, the babies and jam jars and peaches from the front tree and this year finally the figs. I want it all—the sideboard, the antique mantel, the optician's equipment, the plein-air paintings, the tools, the copper pans, the hostas and cyclamen and agapanthus. Sonja says stop. She says stop cramming up the rooms, give some to the kids, but I can't stop, can only stop the pounding in my chest when I stand for a moment before going out the door and count up the plants growing to the edge of the greenhouse, the rugs now piled thick on top of one another, the rare and the ragged, playing their geometric patterns off against one another.

What I can't do, even after my now half days at the office and my regular tennis matches with Jay and even riding the bike around the pond, is sleep. *No sleep for the wicked*, Jay says. I wish more of them lived nearby. Instead they've taken on careers in other cities calling home to report on Chicago's architecture, the movement of the film business to Canada, the cost of apartments in Manhattan. I've bought a new rug in acid green, horsemen buried in the edges, holding up spears and running around the periphery. The days are full in July. Sonja sits in the garden. But I can't, can't sit or read as I used to. Now only the news in brief, only the stories of refugees, moving from place to place, restless, unhoused. All they own left behind, one parcel, one bag. And I can't sleep. The edges of the room are filled with hands gesturing to music, moving in the air. My heart pounds and ribbonlike shadows run along the floorboards.

In the side room at the museum, there are drawings of the bony and veined hands of men, lifting, falling. I turn on the light and look at my own hands, the veins prominent, age spotting the skin. Sonja sleeps early and late, falling asleep in front of the TV, sleeping past nine until she's up to walk the dogs, gathering gossip from the neighbors, paying the gardener and napping under quilts piled at the foot of the bed. It's not that I worry about anything in particular. It's not that I have bad dreams.

GLASS GRAPES

I drove her to the wedding those many years ago. She, Sam, wearing gray and scribbling in a notebook as she was always scribbling things, taking notes, writing aperçus. What a waste, I thought, she could have a life and in the moment I thought that I could be it, but like all that happened to her then and later, I was, I realized, more imagined than real. Not that she lacked all affection, but it seemed the affair was imagined, the ways we sat together reading *Anna Karenina* aloud were imagined, something she couldn't grasp but only pass through—a scene in a play, some occasion for which she invented lines, remembered, replayed. She'd make a garden, if she ever thought to make one, without color or flowers. Sonja comes into the room with flowers, with branches of pussy willow, with gifts wrapped in pale tissue, with another find. *Look*, she says, *I just picked it up on my way home,* and I look at the colors on the glass plate as she holds it up to the light—pink figures dancing around a maypole.

It is night. My calf muscles cramp. Too many games of tennis, I tell myself, wait until Wednesday to play again. My neighbor recommends bone meal. I want morning to come and the world to start up, hate the loss of what is collected on the table under the lamp, what would show up if I turned on all the lights and flooded the shadows, edged the particulars. I want to run my fingers on the velvet upholstery, to hold the ancient bowl and feel its underbelly of soot.

Why does one think of strangers one doesn't really know. Samantha, Sam with her boyish head and niggardly

152

Hands

ways, hands so frail as to seem useless. They fluttered about my shoulders those many years ago until I held them just to get them to lie down flat. They gestured, unsettled and ill at ease, reaching for something, picking up a pencil to scribble. Once Anna's child wanted to go to the aviary at the zoo; birds and butterflies alighted on our shoulders and in our hair. I was twenty again and Sam's hands fluttered in stripes of henna, yellow, the pollen from the iris running across the back of a cat. Why should I think of her, imagine colors on her frail hands, her silly ways, her sad and wasted life. Her handwriting was spindly, fine, peaked as her hair. I wanted to wrap her hands in turban cloth, to buy her something.

Why can't I sleep, I ask myself at breakfast and vow to cut back on wine and red meat, to exercise more and get the gears fixed, to pick up those green glasses Sonja wants on my way home. The light comes in the window and the coffee comes up in the espresso pot and I burn my fingers lifting the scalding milk. Last week at dinner we all ordered the Merlot we had last night and toasted the now pregnant Cely and looked forward to another addition to the clan. Today I celebrate with a stack of new shirts from Filene's basement and I remember the green glasses. But Sonja's not home and the present seems heavy in my arms. The note reads: *Gone to be with Cely. Will call tonight. Back tomorrow. Xxx. S.*

How are you, she said, for there she was ringing me up on the phone. *Where have you come from, Sam*, I said, putting the green glasses on the counter. *I'm in town*, she said, *for Tina's wedding and on my way to a meditation retreat* or a something I didn't catch, not that I didn't hear the words just that it seemed so adolescent, Californian, typical. What irritated me so about her? Even her goodness was irritating, her hours spent sitting at the side of the sick and dying, her poorly paid job at the hospice, her certitude. Fussy, I thought. *How are you*, she said, in a way that always made me think she was laughing at me, at us, at all of us now about to be gathered again under the tent with the glasses of champagne. *I can't sleep.* Now why did I tell her that. So I hurried on, *I just bought a Volvo, deep red and chromey, you'd like it*, I said. What did I care whether she liked it or not. I hadn't seen her since when, since Charlie's illness four years ago when she came to town to sit at the hospital bed, ghoulish attraction to death I thought. *Could we meet for coffee*, she asked. *How are the children? Sonja? Blooming*, I said, *blooming. We're all blooming. Why not come by for dinner—I'll just dash to the store at the corner; we've got veggies in the garden; just come, it's a perfect time.* She only had two hours she said, but she'd come.

At night the quiet is edged by dreams. My father a lolling head, my father without memory, without words, his hands worrying the sheets, signaling to someone standing behind me, someone not there. His face now only a photograph, cheeks tinted a rosy pink. But in the dreams we are held for a moment in a geometric

Hands

shape that is unbearably meaningful but so abstract
that I can't quite see it. I start. I stare into the lamplight.
Every night my father is there mouthing words I can't
hear. I smell the antiseptic corridor, see the thin ties
on his hospital gown.

She's as thin as ever. Seems as if she could blow
away in the wind. Her haircut is worse than ever, one
ear is pierced with four earrings—a woman her age.
And the fingers all have silver rings. What can she be
thinking, I wonder. *I've been thinking of you*, she says.
She's only drawn to those in need, I think, and how
could she—she who is so clearly needy herself—see me
in that light? *I'm so glad to see you*, she says.

As the day faded, they sat in the kitchen, he making a
salad and grilling a bluefish, she drinking iced tea. He
poured himself another glass of Merlot. He felt drawn
to her and to the night he feared, and, unsettled by
this, he tried to give her books he'd collected, but she
said she couldn't carry them, was off to a meditation
center, wanted only the one knapsack. Despite her
size she looked strong enough, but he demurred and
offered wine now he was on to a new bottle. She shook
her head and pulled her own chopsticks out of her
backpack. I like to carry them, she said. How could
she have come to this, he thought, carrying her own
utensils around like some sort of hippy and piercing
her ears and carrying knapsacks like a child on her

way to school. And why did he want to reach out and touch her head, her skull beneath her feathery hair, this sexless creature he had once slept with, laughed with, teased, seen as like them all.

After they ate they sat in the dim light and he for some reason unavailable to him didn't want her to go. I have to go now, she said. I always go to bed before ten. I'll see you tomorrow at the wedding. I can't sleep, he said. Why did he tell her this. It slipped out of him. She put her hands over his. She looked as if she were seeing something as clearly as he could see through the glass slides. They fluttered at first as he remembered and then were still. That was it. She put her hands on top of his. He felt oddly pinioned and even more oddly released. Then she left. That night he dreamed he was in a garden. It was abstract and unrealized, but quiet and still, and he slept and dreamed it all night long.

Like Visiting Joseph Cornell

Surrealism's philosophy relative to, concern with, the "object"—a kind of happy marriage with my life-long preoccupation with things. Especially with regard to the past, a futile reminiscence of the Mill notion that everything old is good & valuable—mystical sense of the past—empathy for antiques—nostalgia for old books.

—Joseph Cornell

He floats, she thought, as she thought about him and she couldn't help thinking about him, out to flea markets, and returns, not with a small glass bottle, but with giant chests of drawers, bent calipers for measuring skulls, an oversized set of scales, a hodgepodge of stuff, most too large to be placed on a table, and so, like everything piled here and there, in the way of legs and feet. Coming here was, she thought, like bumping into a material version of what she wanted, meeting up with things that she couldn't have imagined or couldn't have summoned up the energy to go find, haul into place, pay for, but which once there seemed as familiar as rooms one lay in as a feverish child, the roses on the wallpaper melded in feverish heat. Visiting was like reaching out in the dark to encounter her dead mother on the way to the kitchen to get a glass of water, the hallway between dreaming and waking that as a child she'd taken for granted as another realm in and of itself.

In this one house in Quincy, something of this returned, at least around the edges. There was the pleasure of revisiting the familiar, odd things he'd collected: the 19th-century wooden mantelpiece, the photograph with the smeared emulsion of brooms, the etching of ships coming into harbor. And there was always the pleasure of seeing and touching new objects recently carried in, the anticipation of a future in which there would be more. Her hands opened and shut as if she were being touched instead of touching. It was the house she'd always thought she'd live in and although now she knew she wouldn't, she wanted to visit it as if it would help some transition not only into a past which she didn't want to lose sight of, but also into a future that seemed recently more obscure than ever. Lately the constriction in her lungs seemed to be tightening around more than her lungs. She once came close to moving in when for a moment both of them were off balance—he divorced and she alone. She had taken time off work to spend the summer with him and help paint the shutters. But for some reason hidden now in the past and in all that had happened since, she hadn't.

Like Visiting Joseph Cornell

She said this to the man on the plane. "There must have been more to it," she confessed as people confess high in the air, but somehow her memory had locked onto one scene. She saw herself sitting in the kitchen with him and his now dead mother, anxious about a plane ride back to the west coast and to whatever was going to happen to her. There didn't seem to be a discussion at the center of whatever decision had been made, or whatever decision had occurred, since she couldn't call up a single conversation about it, just those green and pink fringes of anxiety that erupt from a missing center like steamers of confetti falling from the sky.

Her help with the shutters wasn't all. The move into the house was an excavation into someone else's past, their own being too familiar, too ill-defined. If the idea of self-examination ever came up, it was set off to the side, cordoned off. In the dreams she had upon arriving, she found herself trespassing, trying to extricate herself from entangling fences, coming upon flat sheets of cardboard that required intricate fitting together, tabs and slits, but she fumbled—all hands—and woke up. In the decaying house they came upon ruins that drew and transfixed them: bits of melted fiberglass like sculpted embryos, cast ceramic coverings for the wiring, one layer of Victorian wallpaper on top of another: yellow roses, then stripes, then a delicate patterning of small bouquets tied with ribbons, layered like kimono robes one on top of the other as they were unevenly stripped away. The whole room unfolded in a paper fan of green wavy stripes, the wallpaper just put on, 1910: music playing, sun slanting through the tall windows, children waiting to be told.

On some days after a rush of work, they simply stood there, caught in a past life that was more their own than the one before them, as if they could fall asleep and awake, posed formally before the photographer who disappeared beneath a black cloth and ordered them to stand still. The faded photograph of a couple hung in the hallway; the woman's eyes were half closed. In their fatigue, words seemed to take flight, leaving them behind with what felt like hands enlarged and hot from having been slept on too long.

In the dream she had during the second week, he took her to the edge of the sea to a tent. Inside they played volleyball in miniature since the tent was barely large enough for two army cots. She stood on one side of the pushed-together cots and he on the other and they hit the ball back and forth. When she lay down next to him, she felt the hair on his chest like the fur of animals. On the beach were striped umbrellas, children, colored balls and flying Frisbees. This dream, she thought, was somehow an offering of a kind of life they could have or had had as children, but it was very damp and the quarters were so close she felt herself unable to breathe. She remembered her mother telling her that as she had aged her dreams had become unbearably real.

Like Visiting Joseph Cornell

They put on overalls and gloves and face masks and she tied a bandana around her hair to keep out the dust. Their hand tools became extensions of the hands that ached at the end of the day and refused to uncurl easily around a glass of water, a cup of tea, but once in place, latched on, as the cup became a hand, the hand a cup. They had become one entity working on the house, sanding and painting and waiting. She couldn't recognize him in his wrappings, and he couldn't recognize her. Or rather, it wasn't a question of recognition, but of having agreed as they couldn't agree on anything else, to work on this house, to put off, perhaps, a time that would eventually come. They were side by side during the day and into the evening; they were lifting their arms; they were crouching by the molding; they were looking at paint samples, fanning out blues and green-blues and narrowing themselves into corners. When they turned into one another by accident, it was like running into something overly familiar but out of place.

They stripped away broken plaster to the wooden slats beneath. Dust stuck to her. Her hair seemed made of filaments. Her nails tore. Something was caught between her teeth. She couldn't find her socks, her feet, where her feet ended in shoes, the shoes on the carpet, the carpet, dusty and moldy on the wooden floor. They ripped up the carpet, rolled it, took it out to the edge of the street. The window in the bedroom was shifted to the left to give a view to the garden; this shift took days and took it out of her as if parts of her own body had

had to be shifted as well. She was sometimes so tired that she simply lay down on the floor and felt the wood beneath her hands anchor her in place.

At the end of the day they sat across from one another over takeout at the one clean space, the kitchen table, and stared into space. She didn't sleep with him, not only because they were both too tired, but also because they found the intense intimacy of the day, working beside one another for hours, and what turned out to be the unrelenting intimacy of silence over the table, as much as they could take. The Victorian ceilings were high and hard to reach. The inside top shelves of the closet had to be cleaned. The books smelled of foxing. She felt for him in her sleep. Her hands groped the air.

In her dream of the third week he put a yellow dog and her large litter of pups in the bed. They scrambled around on her covers, one paw slipping into a crevice, one ear brushing her face. Everything was lumpy and wet and she felt the bed rock on the waves of the ocean beneath her. The pups dissolved into transparent embryos pulsing their blue veins beneath watery skin. They pushed against her, nudging her, kneading her, licking her.

Crates arrived with the heads of Italian angels, old stone jars, elephants holding up platforms, intricately carved wooden eagles, one with a fish in its mouth. A wooden gazebo from Indonesia filled what used to be the garden lawn. All these objects turned the house into something foreign and exotic, as if a house once landlocked had begun to float, as if the center of the house were no longer just inside, but inside out along the periphery—the porches and patios and gazebos in the yard. The afternoon light was slanted and the air was humid. Horseflies and mosquitoes edged around her hairline. The meadow grasses and Queen Anne's lace invaded the side yard.

It felt like summer, a summer that had disappeared from her vocabulary until now. She took off her overalls and sat in the sun that flickered in the manner of an old film, the faces of the young parents disintegrating in grainy memory. Each segment of the past hour was so etched and shimmering that she felt it would take her years, given the inevitable passage of time, to remember every small detail, the rigging on the painted ship, the warriors and lances in the carpet, the blank marble eyes of angels, the faces in the film. She must, she thought, remember it all. She tilted her face into the bluish haloes of too much sun.

Workmen came and went. She walked about touching the furniture, rubbing shins against the plush of the sofa, the drip of the palm branches, the doorjambs. She took Polaroids of each stage of progress. The odd color of the prints, the muted green wash, seemed to match her sense of the air inside the house that fell on them, and each day they edged closer to retreat from the world outside the walls they worked in, lived in, slept in. The morbidity of the future had, she thought, been finally resolved: it no longer pulsed as before, but had been edged out by the house itself, by its antique trappings, by summers of childhood, and by an agreement that had come into being without their having had to speak of it. There were but two of them. They curled up together suddenly. They slipped glances in between stacks of drawers that fit no bureaus. Their hands met over newspapers that had been left behind and hauled into the kitchen. He read from a scrap of paper, "Sweet hours have perished here; This is a mighty room; Within its precincts hopes have played—Now shadows in the tomb." *Do you remember,* she said, *we first were together when my mother was dying. We sat on the bed in my old room, waiting.*

In the heat of the sun, the air wobbled. Behind her the wallpaper was warm, beating like a heart when she put her hand to it. She reached out to take his hand and licked it as she once remembered doing as a child marking up her room with wet kisses and feeling the toys painted on the slippery wallpaper now imprinted on her tongue.

Part 3

The Letter

If in a letter to you I quote a section from a book I am reading, is the section I am quoting different because it is now filtered through my voice? How is this passage changed, if it is, by being inserted in the context of my letter to you? Does it come to have a significance, even an intimacy, which it would not have if you had bought the book yourself and marked the identical passage? And what if my inclusion of the quotation was meant to imply that it had some bearing on something I had not been able to mention to you for reasons of reticence, but which now I was trying to make known?

Simply by its taking up space on the page, does it impress itself on you despite the fact that you don't read it with care? Or if you skip it altogether, glancing at the page in a cursory fashion as you are apt to do given the constraints on your time, my effort to say something intimate to you in elegant, borrowed language is thereby foiled. I would have chosen a passage I had thought might convey to you how I

think I would write to you if I had the skills of this particular
author, and yet this would have meant nothing to you.

So that after a week or so when I haven't heard from
you, I'll conclude that the passage was offensive to you,
and that I had broken all bonds between us, inserting
language and imagery not my own into so deeply per-
sonal a letter, and that it was not the specific nature of the
material, but rather, the stealing of another's perceptions
in order to convey some semblance of my own that had
ruined everything.

1. If after a time she became wary of her own
tendencies to alter the truth in small and insignificant
ways, but ways which nevertheless she saw as a type of
wickedness, then she felt she had no other recourse but
to quote from others, not that she thought the quoted
material more reliable, but only that it came from
other mouths, not less tainted perhaps, but at least not
her own. And it had been in print: the quoted material
had already been published and had been, therefore,
subject to various reviews and had been corrected by
various editors who were more knowledgeable than she
and capable therefore of saying more about the truth
of things.

So she stitched together letters which for her mattered more than the so-called obvious signs of love, and
sent them to him whether he was nearby and accessible
by phone or had traveled to another city. Wherever he
went there was always a letter waiting for him in which

he looked in vain for a fragment of her natural way of talking, for some expression he recognized, some habit of speech, a private aside.

But there was nothing. Although the letters had begun innocently enough with a few quoted passages, to indicate what she was reading or to reiterate a point, they proceeded to those in which only the introductory salutations were her own, and these were as neutral and official sounding as she was able to make them, as if she were even then, in so momentary a lapse into "her own voice," dependent on a text, polite but distant. Of late, even the introductory statements such as "from an article on optical illusions" or "from the recent essay on portraiture" were excised and only the quotations in all their naked glory were left, and often without punctuation or quotation marks so that the paragraphs from all the articles and newspapers and books ran together like bodily fluids and it was impossible for him to find anything idiosyncratic, anything addressed specifically to him from her in the whole of the letter and yet she insisted she had never so thoroughly poured her heart out to anyone before.

2. Her sense was that only the oblique could convey what she wanted to convey. If one of her photographic subjects stared out directly into the lens, she knew she had failed to capture the true image, that all she would have would be an imitation snapshot like those which filled family albums in which wooden figures

stand squarely before the camera, look into the lens and smile the smile everyone recognizes as "the smile for the camera." Her motto, "never look at the camera," was therefore carried as well into her letters. Her model for this capturing of the truth was the photograph of Dauthendey with his wife: *She is seen beside him in the photograph; he holds her; her glance, however, goes past him, directly into an unhealthy distance.* So, she thought, the wife was captured revealing the future which at the time of the photograph was unrealized by any in the room but for the oblique glance into "an unhealthy distance." The future was caught in the emulsion, not by human insight, but by a random mechanical process.

Yet it was difficult to hold off from the restless, but ever-so-human effort to predict the future. Therefore, she abandoned the quotations themselves and pasted in photographs instead, not of herself gazing romantically into some unhealthy distance, but of those who might be plausible stand-ins for herself and for that which she might wish to say if she knew what that were. The "stand-ins" were most frequently, however, figures with little obvious resemblance to her own person, unless one were to focus on small and almost insignificant details and unless one were adept in ways that seemed even to her to put too fine a point on the matter. And yet, of course, in some way, it was such "putting" that she was after, some way of making him see how she was "like" the image she had substituted for herself, and more importantly, to see how she had so finely predicated what she finally was to come to be, in essence that is, and what, although no one could have seen it coming, was to come to pass.

Of the countless movements of switching, inserting, pressing, and the like, the 'snapping' of the photographer has had the greatest consequences. A touch of the finger now sufficed to fix an event for an unlimited period of time. The camera gave the moment a posthumous shock, as it were.

3. Her focus shifted to the future and she began sending him letters not only full of reference to books she was reading, but also designed to arrive when he would not be home, letters, that is, which he would not receive until later or which, since she often picked up his mail for him when he was out of town, she herself would get upon her return before he did. Thus in some sense these became letters or postcards not to him, although he did ultimately see them stacked up on his living room piano, but to herself, since she would read them over and stack them up for him to read after she had, after his return.

Why does one want to penetrate a time, she thought, unavailable to one at the moment, to insert oneself into the future, to be certain, for example, of one's existence at his house on August 16, although it is at the moment of the writing only August 3. It is "only" the 3RD, she thought, meaning, of course, that the place towards which one was tending was someplace down the road, in a distance one could not see, unless it were captured in some "stroke," some mark on paper or emulsion. To try to visualize herself sitting in his house surreptitiously reading the descriptions of weather on August 3 at a future time, August 16, was like adding days to the week, was like stolen time on a lovers' afternoon, was like the forbidden pleasure of knowing for certain that one would exist at a time not yet come into being, and that she had helped thereby to frame and predict the order of things.

To see her own words written there, *it is raining,* or *it has stopped raining,* was a pleasure that verged on a type of illicit potency, similar one might speculate to the alphabet itself, the way it could hold time as talking could not, and she imagined, the cessation of speech, the pleasure of existing only in the written word, and it was not so much that she wished to exist for him, but rather that she used him as a vehicle by which she could convey herself to herself, that she actually existed and had been wherever she had been and that the rain had been rain, not because she returned with a suitcase full of damp clothes and muddy shoes, but because it was written: *it is raining.* Also and equally satisfying perhaps, because the words in ink on the postcard of a rural landscape were smeared, running slightly down the card or because the card itself, an ordinary shot of rivers and trees, was curled as a card might be, especially a card left for the carrier in a mailbox standing for hours in the pouring rain.

Then she would hold it, standing as she was at a later time, by the piano in the lamplight, and realize that she actually had been where it was raining, and that she had, moreover, successfully projected herself into the room in which she was standing, had (having imagined it and photographed it in her mind's eye—*figure in room with postcard in left hand*) brought it into being. And she felt a sense of prescience which nothing else, things far more momentous and significant in terms of what are called "life events," could provide, nothing but her own words on the cardboard on the flipside of which a landscape in fake fall colors which she had never seen, shone in all its gaudy autumn glory.

4. What she wanted to do was create in him a desire for herself, but herself purified and expunged, exquisitely missing. So having gotten him used to reading quotations which she included in all of her letters, eventually, she cut them out. At first, she did this by cutting sentences and inserting the requisite dots (...) to indicate that some portion of the text was missing. Rarely did this change the meaning of the quotation; more often it simply served to smooth and "get to the main point" more quickly. Later, she took to cutting out the topic sentence or the sentence which, if he had been adept, he would have picked as the one, although not central to the quoted text itself, central to her, central not in any obvious or crass sort of way, but central to

her understanding of what she might become given the ideal projections of her talents and predilections.

After more time had passed, the whole was composed of mere fragments and gaps. From a certain perspective and from a rather sophisticated one, the bits and fragments seemed to compose a sort of poetic assemblage, or at least she, assuming that he was missing her acutely, found it intriguing to imagine that he might find them so. Ultimately, she "cut" all the words out of her letters so that what was left was a piece of blank paper which hung together by threads, rather like the paper dolls which are connected by a thin strip of hands linking them across the accordion pull-out of their fates before being tossed in the fire. And since it became quite difficult to fold them neatly into an envelope, even a business envelope of more considerable size, she stuffed them into the envelope crudely and mailed them off rather unconscious of the mangled wad that would be retrieved on the other end. She imagined that he would pull out a perfect frame of paper, decipher the shape of the missing quotations, and even, in the rather hallucinated state of longing, be able to guess at her underlying intention and embrace the nature of things between them.

5. The letter itself became for her a kind of rival in love, not the means by which she wrote to him, not the link and conveyer of information which would maintain contact over the time they were necessarily apart,

The Letter

enabling her to call up his image and imagine the time when they would be together at last again, but rather that which she most looked forward to. The upcoming time when they had planned to meet completely faded in her imagination and she found herself delaying her return so that she could continue to write to him. Each day she worked quickly to complete the tasks that were at hand and that fulfilled her professional obligations in order to have the leftover moments in which she could turn to writing to him. Thus in the course of her stay in the country, what were to have been moments of snatched time, the rag-ends of time in which she might, if she had time, write to him just to keep him up to date and to assure him of her affection and her certain return, became in flip-flop, a negative to a missing positive, that which she most looked forward to and treasured.

Yet there were days in which, she found, despite writing to him, that she could not remember what he looked like, could not call up the color of his eyes. She tried to remember his image and pulled out, as anyone would do in such circumstances, a photograph of him she had tucked into the back of a book she had been reading when she left, but for some reason the face in the photograph in no way matched what fragments of him she thought she could remember and even less seemed to match the image of the man to whom she had been writing. He wasn't a complete stranger, of course. She realized that the man in the photograph was someone she had once known and she remembered his name, address, profession, quirks. But as to that memory that fills in the bare outline, *that* was completely missing. There was no feeling of animosity towards the man; it was simply that he had lost the limbs of familiarity and had become not an intimate, but someone she had once known. For a time she thought the photograph was to blame, that it was a poor likeness, taken from the wrong angle, or capturing—as photographs do from time to time—a fleeting expression that although quite uncharacteristic of the person being photographed, passed across his face and was fixed by the camera for all time, as if the person were turned into a caricature of himself, not what he was at all, but more like his opposite, not exactly an evil twin, but a shadowy figure with a hidden past.

6. Having realized this fact, she saw that somewhat like DNA is a snapshot in miniature of the whole person, so his face, or at least the top half of his face, was (if separated from the rest) dimly familiar and welcome. If she placed a piece of paper over the rest of his body, especially over his mouth, and looked only at his eyes and brow, she remembered in a vague way that she knew him and had known him well.

Therefore, once she had finished with work on one particularly overwrought day, she took this flimsy snapshot, the only one she had brought with her, to the local camera lab to have it blown up. She had in mind to select a manageable portion, a quotation, as it were, from the larger book of life itself. With the grease pencil, she outlined the square which she wanted and said she would pay and wait. It would be auspicious, she thought. This action was the best she had thought of yet. It was a way to enlarge, down to the pores and dots, that bit which was familiar, reassuring, her own. It was better than future time; it was stop-time altogether. For, she reasoned, with some controlled but obvious excitement, the further one went inward, the more intimate all would become.

Thus, whatever distance might have developed between them would be warded off by the increasing enlargement of the eye in the photograph, and, given what she believed to be her genuine desire for reparation, she had it enlarged until first only the eye and eyelid were visible and then finally only the pupil itself, round and black and firmly situated as if it were looking back at her through the lens of a camera, magnified and clear. The pupil was a firm black spot, a perfect circle. She moved in and in on it, both by the technical process of enlargement and by imaginative endeavor. She was so far in finally that there was no longer any way to conceive of the discrete letters or images which had haunted her all summer. All was blackness: a relief, a refuge, a familiarity so profound as to be unnerving, as if, she thought in the midst of staring, once the envelope was closed and sealed, addressed to the man to whom she would eventually send it, she was no longer on the outside, but, blissfully, surrounded by the blackness at which she focused and to which she was able, finally, to give herself completely, on the very inside itself.

The Photograph

*The objective nature of photography confers on it a quality of
credibility absent from all other picture-making. In spite of any
objections our critical spirit may offer, we are forced to accept as
real the existence of the object reproduced, actually, re-presented,
before us.*

—Andre Bazin

When she arrived at his house after some days
alone, she moved awkwardly and started sentences at
the front door which began in an artificial and stilted
register. Whatever intimacies of their affair had been
in the air were gone. She couldn't see where the skin
of his face might meet hers if she leaned towards him,
so she backed into the kitchen in a kind of awkward
dance, having made certain to bring in bags of groceries
for their usual Friday night dinner so that their bodies
would be occupied in carrying, lifting, unpacking. She
folded the shopping bags along their creases and made
a comment that was meant to sound polite.

She seemed stripped of memory, her body gone neutral and suspicious, as if she hadn't spent nights in his bed. She was, she was proud to say, a skeptic, sophisticated in her sense of how deeply time affected all emotional connections. I am, she thought, someone who has been through more and I am certain of this as he cannot possibly be, living here in this suburban house with the pastel wall-to-wall carpeting, what can he know about how people betray one another. I have only, and she thought this somewhat smugly, taken up with betrayers, and she counted them. She tried to explain to him that everything always changed and that he wouldn't, once time had passed, think of her in the same way ever again.

It turned out he never quarreled and when there were differences between them, usually slight, he sat under the Chinese lamp by the stone fireplace to talk about them and see where they would get to. Despite this, she found herself unable to give up the habit of opposition. That she geared up for argument, walking about the room, crossing and uncrossing her legs, superstitious and unwilling to let go any advantage, seemed to matter to him not at all. He simply went to the corner of the large room, sat down under the Chinese lamp, and waited for her to say something. She made up a story. Last night, she said, she had been at dinner with two friends who were going to China. They had eaten knotted tofu. It was the Chinese lamp that set her going this time, she realized after two sentences in, but by then it seemed so plausible and was after all analogous to the truth (she had eaten tofu one night last week) that it sounded, as specific information tends to, true.

On the lamp were fading figures of monks climbing up a faded mountain, a craggy line that jagged up the porcelain. The lamp was old, had belonged to his mother whose second husband had been a missionary, and he had inherited it along with, oddly enough, the posture of his stepfather. No genes, just the crook of their backs and the quiet of their voices. The story of the Chinese restaurant came out of her mouth in a line of sentences that seemed plausible; the paragraph made a certain amount of sense and avoided, so she hoped, clichés. Clichés were far worse than lying. Indeed, lying seemed these days not only interesting but closer to something she was trying to get to. It reproduced a kind of etched reality, like a photograph of a crime scene that could catch the clues the scene itself would obscure.

Sometimes she thought she was trying to get close to childhood. Didn't psychologists speculate that childhood was a placeholder for authenticity? Ironic, she thought. She looked at a snapshot of herself as a ten-year old. She had never looked at the camera and she never, so far as she could remember, told what she believed to be the truth, although the adjustments were so small as to be undecipherable and, more importantly, completely ir-relevant. The pact of honor she made with herself was that none of her lies should count for anything, should bring her any gain, should hurt anyone, and they didn't, she thought, unless the act itself counted as transgression, but she thought or rather hoped, not. Perhaps her parents always knew she was making things up. Perhaps the little games she played were not of the consequence she had thought them, but simply the insignificant games of children. The gap between what was going on and what she said was going on seemed enormous at the time, but perhaps not.

What words might there be for a child of nine for the mixture of emotions she felt when she watched her little brother move slowly from room to room. His head was too large for his body and he moved with maddening if rather graceful attention to his efforts as if without that attention to his foot pointing forward into the next step, he might wobble, though he never lost his balance and he never fell. She, on the other hand, ran from room to room, sped through corridors, smashed up elbows and shins. She watched him as if he were a gelatinous being from a far-off world she could never inhabit.

Her feelings about all this did not present a moral problem exactly, but neither was it a problem simply of movement. When she had said to her brother, *Come with me*, knowing that he would and that he would move in his slow underwater way with his feet pointing out towards the space in front of him, it was a false premise really, a denial, since she didn't mean *come*, but more like *stop, who are you, why do you do that?* But her brother would simply come as if she had said the simplest thing in the world, whereas she knew that it was not.

The Photograph

The man she sat next to on the couch by the Chinese lamp moved this way as well, with slow and quiet attention to his movements as if the air were thick. She looked at him and tried to remember what it had been like two nights ago in the warmth of his bed, but time had betrayed her and she couldn't remember a thing. She looked at him, his head always bigger than she remembered. Sometimes she wanted to bang up against him as he moved from room to room to jolt him out of his reverie, to see if she could find out something. Sometimes she wanted to move so quickly that he would be forced wide awake, his hair standing on end and glistening.

She kept a photograph of her brother in her wallet and took it out to show him. *Come here and look at this,* she said and he did. The man in the photograph had indeed a quite large head, beautifully shaped with hair long and flat enough to curl around his ears. He looked as thoughtful as a mathematician ought to look. *I bought him that Batman tie for his twenty-first birthday*, she said. It was, however, despite the seemingly obvious evidence at hand, not her brother but a man who was not the first but the most skillful of her betrayers. She carried it in her wallet and always said it was her brother although she didn't know why since it wouldn't have mattered to anyone who it was and she needn't have ever opened her wallet to anyone except for purposes of identification to clerks who didn't, of course, care. Even the man himself under the Chinese lamp wouldn't have cared or wouldn't, even if he had thought of it, have asked why she had the photograph and what it meant. But that was for her the point: its meaning was contained in its lack of meaning, its very ordinariness and banality. She had helped make it more than that, she would have argued, by the additional fillip of the lie. The man looked slightly to one side of her face and listened, as he always listened, to her talk. He took the photograph in his hands and pushed his hair behind his ears.

A lie seemed, she thought, although she couldn't explain why, less intrusive than the truth, less insistent because less obviously connected to the world. It was lighter than air and therefore, like words which in no way corresponded to the things themselves, *perfect*. From time to time she thought she was being cruel—not dishonest, since that seemed a concept so difficult to define that she simply brushed it to the side—but perhaps, she thought, perhaps cruel. He might think, as she was certain she wasn't, that she was purposefully lying to him for some reason, but it was simply her way of showing him the nature of the world, of providing him a way of seeing more clearly or around corners.

You must understand, she said, returning to her usual point, *that things won't always be the same; you won't always, as I am sure you must know, be glad to see me or miss me when I am not sitting here next to the Chinese lamp. Things are always changing, and just because something seems fixed, it might, one day, be quite otherwise. I mean, for example, you know,* and she sounded, even she knew, preachy, *things aren't always what they seem—even photographs are doctored, you know, they simply scan them in and erase whatever they don't want for the story or whatever. They take things out and put things in.* He sat quietly listening to her and she found herself telling him that when she was a child her parents had needed to tame her speed, her *hyperactivity* they called it, and had thrown her against the wall. She looked over at him to see if he believed her. *Yes,* she said, *they took me by the shoulders and threw me against the wall. I rocked myself to sleep in a corner, humming and banging my head on the wall.*

When she had been in her twenties she spent time looking at photographs of autistic children who didn't make eye contact, who refused to speak, who banged their heads against the wall. She remembered clearly how it had felt but she didn't know if remembering made it true. It hurt some, but in truth that was nothing compared to the relief of hearing a steady and rhythmic sound that blotted out everything else. What was *everything else,* she wondered now, and what was wrong with those children that they had to muffle up the world with so odd a manner of rocking, swaying, banging. Now that she had told him she also told him that the person she was describing, the child she had in tow, seemed more like a character in a book than herself. *It was so very long ago,* she said, *it can't really be true, but simply a story I have made up.*

The man sat quietly and listened to her. He felt, so it seemed to her, no great need to comment on these stories of her childhood, or for that matter, to analyze their meaning, their relation to him or even to her. He heard every word she said, but he didn't need, as she certainly did, to make them make sense or to fit them into his sense of her, whatever that might be. He always said he was glad to see her when she returned for the weekend with bags of groceries, but she wondered what it might mean since she had told him so many stories that there was no way for him to know who she really was. What did he see when he looked at her and how, she wondered, could she manipulate his seeing without his knowing she had done so, and how would she want, in any case, to look.

She told him she had been a photographer, *in a former life*, but what she didn't tell him was that it was her brother who had been the photographer and that the photographs she passed off as her own were ones she had taken from him. She entertained him, or at least believed she did, with stories about Nadar's portrait photographs, their deliberate solidity, the way the folds of a person's skin were like the marbled folds of the curtain in the background. *We can't help it*, she said, *we just can't help believing that what's in a photograph is real, no matter what.*

She gave him a photograph of herself to put on his bedside table, a photograph that made her look completely *natural*—unposed, uncropped, undramatic. She did not look especially good or even as good as she might have looked if she had chosen more carefully. Yet in truth,

The Photograph

she had had many photographs of herself taken and had torn up most and chosen not the one that showed her at her best, but the one that seemed most randomly selected, as if it were just left over or just the one she happened to find lying about to give him. She was looking out into space and her face was slightly, although only slightly, blurred as if she were in the early stages of flight. Such a gift, if one could call it a gift, was, she knew, another falsity, although she was as yet unable to name for what. She so wanted to give him something, some iconic disruption that would, so she convinced herself, ultimately please him or reorient him in ways he would surely embrace, if not quite yet. It was the artifice of the unaffected, the pose of the unposed. She had had a purposefully bad haircut, so short she looked like a boy, not unlike her brother at a young age. She said she was afraid he would forget her if he didn't have the photograph to remember her by. *You might forget me*, she said, sitting under the Chinese lamp, knowing all the while that she wasn't telling the truth.

In truth, it was she who would forget him, would forget after a short time what his eyes were like, and would be, therefore, in spite of the ploy of the groceries and the carefully prepared and polite questions, unable to return, and who would tell those who asked that he was, like the others, one of the betrayers who wasn't, she had come to discern and despite appearances to the contrary, at all what he seemed. And she would continue to say to those who still would listen that it was a classic case of betrayal (*You can never tell about appearances, she'd say*) and would, somewhat to her credit, know that it was no such thing.

—❧—

Soft Conversation

Whatever faith exists it will not be altered by human affairs. Those who believe deeply in the Buddha consider it possible that when he arrives the wind and waves will be calmed.

—Inscription in Cave 323, Tang dynasty

Their conversations were always so soft they didn't get anywhere, but then neither did either get really upset or disoriented as happens sometimes when there is direct disagreement or tension between the two parties who are trying to agree about what to do about a specific problem, a hard one, or what should they do in general, even harder. It was as if they had entered into a room lined with soft materials and moved about effortlessly and easily, bumping into one another softly.

The shape of their conversations goes something like: *what do you think,* and *yes I agree with you,* and *I'd be happy to try if you'd like to,* and *you certainly are right.* The entire conversation has a sort of ritualized shape to it, organized around repeated phrases, and a rather respectful even reverential manner. If anyone thinks this is an exaggeration, just try eavesdropping once in a while. It is rather as if what one hears, rather than the individual voices, is a sort of echoing drone, a circling around a central tone of accord.

What is being set in motion by their engaged endeavor at agreement is not however only agreement but rather the process of perpetual becoming, each of them dedicated to the idea, although neither has a need to speak of it, of never reaching a conclusion and thereby slowing time to the eternal present by means of never arriving but always rearranging the terms of the agreement. If one comes into conflict, on the other hand, as they both recognize, one of the parties will win and one will lose and time will be reinstated. It will be 3 A.M. and one of them will exult, *I win*.

But if they keep on having the same or nearly the same conversation about, as it happens this time, a trip they might take in the future, they will possess that trip endlessly since they will never arrive at the moment of decision, will never buy the tickets, will never experience liftoff or jet lag and will never regret that the trip has come to an end.

Thus far they have successfully prolonged time through Thailand, Japan, and China, all places they thought they had wanted to visit and certainly they had read the guidebooks about, wanting especially to encounter what they believed would be a different sense of time, a sense of time slowed and prolonged towards which they aspired. They would, they thought, be encouraged to recognize the transitoriness of all human endeavor and the need to avoid attachments to the paltry things of this world.

She had been especially drawn to the Chinese caves at Dunhuang since time there was layered over itself again and again, walls originally painted in the 4TH century, then repainted in the 6TH and afterwards partially destroyed and repainted until the encrusted present was an emblem of multiple times overlapped into the present moment that they would see once they got there. It was the color she especially wanted, the hallucinated and druggy turquoise of the ceilings and, she thought, it must have helped those long-ago believers touch the eternity they chanted about while circling round and round the center pole. The Buddhist angels floated up there, holding bowls of timelessness in their outstretched hands. This was the trip they had most agreed upon; it seemed to them at the exact moment during which they were discussing it to be the most perfect trip in the world. Their voices grew soft and quiet as they came into perfect accord. The moment seemed to extend. The room fairly hummed with unity and pleasure. It will be perfect, they said.

But of course once they had agreed on the perfection of this specific plan and walked in circles about the living room, saying *yes it seems exactly right,* and *I agree about the length of the stay,* and *what a good idea you've proposed,* they were unable to move out of the perfection they already had in hand. It seemed a travesty to disrupt it. They could see the whole so completely that the thought of leaving this perfection for the imperfection of dusty travel stopped them dead in their tracks. And so they gathered themselves into the agreed-upon rituals of chanted accord. They pulled the caves of their own making in close and agreed that it would be best, *yes*, she echoed, for the time being, not to rush into anything, but to go over the same ground again and again, trying to get a sense of having already been where they had thought to go so that they could finally agree on how much they had thoroughly enjoyed the moment of standing still in the middle of Magao Cave 323 where they could almost hear the distant chanting of believers.

Listening In

She listened to him talking quietly on the phone, although she knew it was something she wasn't supposed to do. She knew that in his former life others had pulled at him and asked him what he was doing, whom he was talking to, when he was leaving, and when he was coming back. Now the unspoken rule between them in this new life they had set up was to walk into the other room and not to.

She could, however, hear him say something in the even way he did no matter what and agitation kicked in. It seemed a reaction one might have to poison oak, although that couldn't be right since this was a non-irritant that made her irritable. How could quietude in a quiet room set her off?

Trying not to respond to someone who most especially wants you not to respond was hard. It seemed a kind of setup if you were the sort of person, surprisingly, she found, she was. It was difficult not to say, *who was that dear*. It was difficult to try not to have a reaction when you were having a reaction and she found that trying not to try was worse.

She found herself lurking in ways she had never lurked before. She hadn't thought of herself as someone who would lurk in the hall, just so she could listen in. She found her own body dragging slowly through the hall and found it hard to recognize herself, she who always had taken her days as they came. She wondered who that person was she had become, the one who listened in.

She had read about men who had secret lives and she was sure he was not one of them. But it was hard to tell despite his obvious integrity. Then too, you could never tell, and she was the one at home alone all day while he went off to teach his classes and although he said they were perfectly matched, it was true she didn't understand the books he wrote. Somehow, despite the lectures she gave herself about it, these phone conversations made her feel left out and, although she had never used the word *alienated* before, it was what she felt.

His conversations were lengthy, quiet, serious. They took place during or after dinner while she was clearing up. She thought she could hear certain repeated words and she tried to piece them together as if she were knitting together an ancient manuscript. There were words she recognized like *emptiness* or *dependent* and there were words that came in a sort of tonal slur so that she couldn't quite get hold. After holding back for sometime she'd sometimes allow herself to ask, in a voice a bit too bright, who had called, but he would smile and say *no one* or *it's nothing important*, not meaning, she thought, in any way to dismiss her question which however he didn't answer as he moved out of the room into his study.

Over a period of time she collected the overheard words in a list and when she typed them into Google she got back any number of sites she thought might be useful in sorting out what was going on in the back of his mind. Pages printed out in front of her and she underlined the important ones in yellow marker:

#1 *Ultimate truth 'cannot be spoken'* **(pu k' e shuo ag)**.

Taking up the idea of the unspoken, she tried to pare down what she said and more often than that to smile blankly during all conversations. It seemed a gesture that was as close to the truth as she could get, especially since her own smile was a bit crooked, one side of a lip sidling up farther than the other. She tried not to push as she had occasionally done previously, but to let things go their own way into silence.

At first she found this unpleasant, like watching a string of words freeze in the air. He continued to make the phone calls as he had always done, although he noticed that their interactions had shifted somewhat. Nevertheless, he had his work to do and he continued to move ahead, phoning, e-mailing, writing, and working. She wasn't sure where this would get them, but she'd see.

She read: *The Bodhisattva's mode of being is described in terms of 'no grasping,' 'no attachment.'* She was unsure what to do since she'd always liked holding onto him, not in public, of course—she hated couples who grabbed each other in public—but in the kitchen on the way through the house, she liked the sense of being attached to him, settled into his skin and clothes, washing them, folding them, a bit of cloth passing under her hands. She decided to leave the laundry until next week.

#2 Conventional truth is **samsara** *in that it alienates one from the source and truth of all existence.*

The word she grasped most clearly and the one that seemed most useful was *conventional*. She knew, of course, that he was the intellectual and she the conventional one. But before she hadn't minded and he seemed to appreciate her willingness to keep life going for them both. She'd do the shopping and he'd go to work. She'd buy the groceries and cook; he'd read academic magazines before dinner and retreat to his study afterwards while she took up her colored pencils to draw.

Listening In

She'd put on her favorite movie and then arrange the pencils in rows and draw precisely accurate pictures of everything in the house as Julie Andrews sang. She had already done the furniture, the items in the refrigerator, the contents of her purse, even the money, the coins and bills, the ticket stubs and credit cards. At first the pictures were not so small, but they began to get so much smaller that she could fit hundreds on a single sheet. As she fitted them one after another in rows across the blank paper, it seemed to make them all equal somehow, as if the large and the small could all be colored red.

She noticed that the unconventional women in the neighborhood tended to go to classes, gardening classes or yoga classes or mommy and me classes. You could recognize them by their footwear. Since she had no children and no garden, this left the yoga class, and so she enrolled in the local Y. Her favorite pose was the corpse pose at the end, but the rest was fine as well and she kept it up. One morning when he had needed to let her know he would be late returning from work, he phoned, but she didn't answer. When he asked her where she had been, she said *nowhere dear.* She thought it would be best if she sprung all her unconventionality on him at once, perhaps for their anniversary coming up soon. She thought that might be the right time.

She hadn't been sure she'd like the classes, they seemed so peculiar and the words so foreign, but she did. It seemed like loading the dishwasher. You had to be adept, you had to be precise, you had to pay attention to each plate and slot. She slotted herself into the sideways facing warrior pose between two panes of glass. She floated in the space like an insect on a flower and, although she'd never felt so alone before, she also felt fine.

One day when her husband couldn't reach her, he came home for lunch and slipped on the wet path up to the front door and twisted his ankle, not too badly, but it did hurt and he had to wear a soft cast. He found himself reaching out for solace in ways he hadn't before.

When the phone rang after dinner, she answered it and then held it at arm's length and waited for him to make his way with his one crutch over to the small space off the kitchen. She found that his sprain made him talk louder into the mouthpiece so that it was easier to listen for the special words, but she had to do the dishes quickly in order to get to the meditation class recommended by her yoga instructor, so she forgot to listen. *Goodbye dear,* she called and left as he was finishing up the conversation on the phone.

#3 Destruction, cessation, non-existence, elimination, exhaustion—all give negative description to the experience of ultimate truth.

The center of truth seemed the most perplexing and painful of all. Moreover and in truth, she and her husband had become completely out of touch and exhausted. He spent all his time writing his book and she spent all her time working on her new spiritual life and when she wasn't working on her spiritual life and taking up new forms, Ashtanga and Flow, she was drawing members of her yoga class. She had given up attention to the things at home—they seemed somehow ghostly, illusory, from some period in her life she couldn't remember—and she became fixated on making a poster of very small figures in all the poses she had been learning.

She wasn't at all sure how to get the feet right, and besides they were so often in places no one's feet were meant to be, and though she hated to admit it, she began to long for Julie Andrews on the hillside. She crumpled paper after paper. She was tired. Late at night they passed on the way to the bedroom, completely devoted to the experiences they were having, but worn and somewhat lonely.

#4 The most important implication of dependent origination, therefore, is that no entity exists independent of other entities.

One morning as she was working with her pencils during yoga class, she realized that she didn't recognize anyone. Her neighbors whom she had known slightly before beginning the class and whom by now she knew far better, seemed like strangers to her. Perhaps, she thought, it was that they assumed such twisted postures, were upside down and backwards, turned into dogs, trees, camels, and ploughs. When she got home, she showered, hoping to wash away the queasy feeling of dislocation, and dried her hair before the mirror, but she found she too had taken on a look she couldn't quite recognize, a look not animal or vegetable, but partial.

When her husband returned late that night, his limp still keeping him to a bit of a slow pace and the use of a cane, she looked at him hard. He too looked partial, partly she supposed because she hadn't seen much of him of late or hadn't looked at him carefully for some time, but partly because he looked smudged as if she had run her thumb across one of the lines of her drawings.

For the first time in months she decided to run a few sentences by him to see how it would go. *How are you,* she asked, *how's your work going, what would you like for dinner tomorrow, did you notice the moon on the way home, what do you think we should do for our anniversary, does your foot hurt much, would you mind fixing the screen door, how's Stan?* Since it had been a while, she simply spun out an entire list, thinking to catch up as it were. He looked startled, but replied, *fine, ok, spinach, yes, go to a movie, yes, I'm afraid so, I'll get to it tomorrow, and not bad, I think.*

It reminded her of the church services of her youth—call and response. When they finally got over the odd shape of this exchange, they both felt better and settled in their skin. It seemed they'd gotten somewhere both familiar and different. That night they hooked into one another in the bed as they hadn't done for weeks and slept better than they had for days. For their anniversary, they went to a movie and out to dinner at a nice local restaurant and had the usual.

———

Page 42

I know I've read the beginning before, maybe last summer. I picked up the book and read some few pages. Now, however, that I'm about a third into it the story still seems familiar to me and I'm wondering if indeed I read exactly this far, or if the unfolding of the story was so obvious that even though I didn't actually get this far before, I could predict that I would recognize the new characters who've been introduced and that I would be as uninterested in continuing to read as I was last summer.

Of course this makes one think about why one wants to read in so beautiful a spot anyhow where there are any number of other things to do: swim, walk, stare at birds. Today I tried staring at the birds, but after a while, no matter that I was also sunning myself, doing two things at once that is, not just one, I found myself wanting to read. The birds were interesting and even predatory, but I couldn't get into it. So I reread the article in the newspaper about the guinea hens which people are keeping on their lawns to eat the ticks that cause lime disease and which people are very glad to have even though the birds make a sound like fingernails on a blackboard and even though their lawns are now full of holes where the guineas have gone after ticks. They are good at it and some feel, so the article says, finally safe though they check their children all over just to make perfectly sure. The whole thing seems rather tedious and the article was endless so I didn't finish it and when I looked up the birds had gone.

So I return to the novel I might have read before and am especially attracted to the dampness of it, the boys lying about in damp bedclothes, the dampness of the city on canals, and the damp eroticism of the novel because it so matches my own situation here in the cabin in which I am damper than ever before and also the towels and dishcloths; and the floor even seems damp under my bare feet because it is summer and I am always walking in bare feet in summer, often with a book under my arm. And the pages of the book turn and curl in the downpours and residual damp. Water drips off the leaves in the woods where the cabin is located. I sit and watch the covers of the paperbacks curl. At night or when I have left the room and then return, I find the cover curled, unless I've remembered to weight it down with other books, preferably hardback books which the current novel is not nor is it hardcore, though as I said, decidedly damp and erotic and so plotless as to seem familiar, as if one read about the boat ride in the canals previously, although now I am sure that last summer I didn't get this far and that the covers were more or less flat.

And of course I feel guilty because I ought to be doing something other than reading, but I can't seem to stop reading except of course when I stop reading to do something equally useless like throw out bread crumbs for the birds and see what comes or fall asleep and into such a deep sleep I am with the boys in the novel throwing off bedclothes in the damp heat and throwing my legs about and scratching the scabs I have gotten from insect bites because of the holes in the screens. At night the moths come in and distract me from reading and sleeping which are the only things I do well except I have begun a list of the different sorts of moths even the ones which have died by morning and look like dried-up brown leaves. So far my favorite is the copperglaze moth, metallic and quite small, about the size of a thumbnail, and it also has the advantage of not flying about much so that in the midst of an unread paragraph one can look steadily and not have it bang into the light which one must have on if one is to get any reading done.

So I return to the book I remember so vividly and yet vaguely and a central narrator with whom I cannot identify in the essentially plotless story and find myself thinking how much his experiences and mine are alike as he tries to pursue his tasks in the midst of increasing dread. It is the dread that does it, the summer dread that is absolutely the worst since it's based on so little information about the sorts of ticks and spiders and moths which surround one and are so simultaneously invisible as one is going blithely about one's business of reading the books one has to read in the course of a summer vacation.

What the narrator seems to dread, I think, is some dissolution into the books he is reading which he feels are encroaching on what used to be his firm sense of identity; he was writing something or doing research on something, but in the midst of all this quiet ordinary endeavor he finds himself feeling a sense of dread from the dangers of the city in which he lives and from an array of unusual circumstances which seem not exactly unusual in any bizarre or outlandish sort of way but just slightly unexpected. And of course I can't really identify with this urban dread since I'm in the woods and have no fear of helicopters flying overhead and shining searchlights into my window, but nonetheless as I read further in the book, I find myself unable to lie about dazedly as I was wont to do. Rather I find myself unnerved, fearing the unnameable something that has leaked into my cabin from this book which I make such poor progress in reading.

Each night as I pick it up before going to bed I find myself having to reread what I had read the night before in order to remind myself of the events which remain, despite the mood of dread, unmemorable, and by the time I have finished reading the portion from the night before I find myself unable to proceed much further, often only a sentence or two, before I drop off to sleep, a sleep which was once untroubled, but which since the taking up of this project of reading the unfinished novel from the previous summer, has been restless, troubled even, I should say. I think sometimes that I ought to get rid of this novel, bury it in the woods perhaps or find a local library and put it in the overnight return slot where someone efficient would in the morning figure out what to do with it. But then I reason with myself that this is an absurd way to behave over a novel, especially one I haven't finished and which might, if I persevere, have a quite rounded and comforting ending, one which would repay all my efforts from last summer and this.

Another possibility would be to take up reading a history of the city in which the central character is located so that in spite of the failure of this particular book I would have nonetheless propelled myself forward. But for some reason this also never happens and again it is evening and I have turned on the lamp and I pick up the novel and open its damp and mildewed pages, pages giving off that vaporish smell of old cabins and foxing. And again the copper moth comes and lands on the top end of the book and again I am filled with the dread of something about to occur, something looming in the distance which I will be unable to fend off, something too vague to get a firm picture of so that I am unable to conceive a plan of attack.

Page 42

In the morning I wake with the light still on, the book fallen as usual to my chest, and the moth dead and stuck to page 42, the page I have reread any number of times during the course of this particular week. And nothing has yet happened really to the narrator, nothing has moved him forward, and he hasn't yet figured anything out. No, he is still doing research and reading in the hopes that one day he will see all things clear, will be able to fall into a damp bed and arise transformed, but as yet he is unable to move beyond p. 42, dependent as he is on my abilities which are for the moment lost, no longer exactly in a swamp of dread, but in the limp sluggishness of being unable to turn to p. 43 on which page it might be that something would finally happen or that he would finally move beyond the reading stage to something else which he can't quite conceptualize, caught as he is in another's inability to finish the novel which seems vaguely familiar as if I have read it all before.

—❧—

Notes

The quotations from Joseph Cornell in the epigraph for the book and in "Like Visiting Joseph Cornell" are from *Joseph Cornell: Theater of the Mind, Selected Diaries, Letters, and Files*, edited with an introduction by Mary Ann Caws, a book about things, obsessions, monologues, and dreams.

"The Watch": The quotation is from Ezra Pound's "The Jewel Stairs' Grievance."

"The Teabowl": In Vermont near Whitingham there is a 25-acre floating island on Sadawaga Pond.

"Old Nylon Bathrobes": Jim Dine's Bathrobe series provides illustrations of bathrobes that suggested to me the complex artificiality of seemingly simple renditions.

"The Tattoo": William Coe's *Tikal: A Handbook of the Ancient Maya Ruins* provides detailed graphic designs of carved monuments, similar to the tattoos imagined in this story. I chose the designs of Mayan ruins because I had read *Mayan Letters* by Charles Olson.

"Glass Grapes": The poem referred to is "The Day Lady Died" by Frank O'Hara.

"His Subject/Her Subject": I quote Wittgenstein on "trying" because his work so pointedly raises the question of how complex the seemingly ordinary can be, and because trying seems so frequently to fail in the face of things one can't understand.

"My Son and the Bicycle Wheel": In "Apropos of 'Readymades,'" Duchamp refers to his selection of various found objects; I quote him because of his reference to his own construction using a bicycle wheel and because for him also objects were tropic, insistent, indifferent to human beings. This story is for Jacob.

"The Ring": The portrait of Madame Gautreau is by John Singer Sargent; his paintings show up in my work often. The "gleam" mentioned in "The Flea Market" was also taken from one of his paintings, *The Bead Stringers*, at the Clark Museum in Williamstown, Massachusetts.

"La Belle Dame": The poem is by Keats; the quotation is one by Roland Barthes from *S/Z* that I came across while reading Marianne DeKoven, "Gertrude Stein and Modern Painting: Beyond Literary Cubism"; I use it to capture some of the sense of the bald man's thoughts as imagined by the narrator.

In "Blue/Green" I finally quote from Merleau-Ponty, here his essay on "Cézanne's Doubt," but throughout I have been influenced by his essays on the interdependency of the subjective and the objective. The poem is "The Garden" by Andrew Marvell.

Several of the stories in Part 3 refer to photographs or essays about them; the idea of the camera giving "a posthumous shock" is from "Some Motifs in Baudelaire" by Walter Benjamin; the reference to Dauthendey and his wife is from his "A Short History of Photography." My story "The Photograph" begins with a quotation from André Bazin's "The Ontology of the Photographic Image."

"Soft Conversation" begins with a quotation from *Cave Temples of Mogao: Art and History on the Silk Road*, edited by Roderick Whitfield, Susan Whitfield, Neville Agnew, a book describing a place I can only wish I had traveled to.

"Listening In" contains references or warped references to essays on Buddhism by Professor Dale Wright, to whom I dedicate the story.

Acknowledgments

Thanks to the editors of the publications in which the following stories first appeared:

American Letters and Commentary: "The Lightbulb";
The Chicago Review: "Cones";
The Denver Quarterly: "Glass Grapes," "The
    Photograph";
Double Room: "Her Subject/His Subject";
Fence: "Marybeth and the Fish";
Hambone: "Tattoo";
The Harvard Review: "Page 42," reprinted in *PP/FF: An
    Anthology*;
Pleiades: "The Gift";
Tantalum: "My Son and the Bicycle Wheel."

For editorial assistance and encouragement, I want to thank those who helped with specific stories: Thaisa Frank, Laurie Lew, Michelle Huneven, Dennis Phillips, and Dyanne Asimow. For unflagging belief in this project and help both textual and otherwise, I especially thank Wayne Winterrowd and Joe Eck. There are many (more than I could list) whose rooms and objects have found their way into these stories: thank you all very much. The suggestiveness of the world comes in many forms; special gratitude to Dale Wright and to my family.

About The Author

Martha Ronk is the author of a number of books of poetry, most recently, *In a landscape of having to repeat* (Omnidawn), winner of the PEN USA best poetry book 2005, and *Vertigo* (Coffee House Press), a 2007 National Poetry Series selection. She is the recipient of a 2007 NEA grant and has had residencies at both the MacDowell Colony and Djerassi. As a Professor of Renaissance literature at Occidental College in Los Angeles, she has written academic articles on Shakespeare, specifically on ekphrasis, an extended verbal description of a visual object.

BOA Editions, Ltd.
American Reader Series

Colophon

Glass Grapes and Other Stories, by Martha Ronk,
is set in ITC Veljovic, a digital font designed by
Jovica Veljovic (1954–), which displays a crisp
precision, as if the letters were cut in stone rather
than drawn with pen and ink.

⸻

The publication of this book is made possible, in part,
by the special support of the following individuals:

Anonymous (2)
Angela Bonazinga & Catherine Lewis
Alan & Nancy Cameros ❖ Gwen & Gary Conners
Peter & Sue Durant ❖ Pete & Bev French
Judy & Dane Gordon ❖ Kip & Debby Hale
Peter & Robin Hursh ❖ Willy & Bob Hursh
X. J. & Dorothy Kennedy ❖ Jason D. Labbe
Katherine Lederer ❖ Rosemary & Lewis Lloyd
Boo Poulin
Steven O. Russell & Phyllis Rifkin-Russell
Chris & Sarah Schoettle ❖ Vicki & Richard Schwartz
George & Bonnie Wallace
Kay Wallace & Peter Oddleifson
Thomas R. Ward ❖ Patricia D. Ward-Baker
Pat & Mike Wilder ❖ Glenn & Helen William

⸻